Sarah Anne Hartford

MASSACHUSETTS, 1651

————— ✦ —————

by Kathleen Duey

————— ✦ —————

Aladdin Paperbacks

For Richard
For Ever

First Aladdin Paperbacks edition April 1996
Copyright © 1996 by Kathleen Duey
Aladdin Paperbacks
An imprint of Simon & Schuster
Children's Publishing Division
1230 Avenue of the Americas
New York, NY 10020

Designed by Randall Sauchuck
The text of this book is set in Fairfield Medium.
Printed and bound in the United States of America
10 9 8 7 6 5 4 3 2 1

Library of Congress Cataloging-in-Publication Data
Duey, Kathleen.
Sarah Anne Hartford / Kathleen Duey.—1st Aladdin Paperbacks ed.
p.   cm.—(American diaries ; #1)
Summary: Twelve-year-old Sarah breaks the Sabbath in
Puritan New England and faces a moral dilemma when
an innocent person is accused in her place.
ISBN 0-689-80384-2
[1. Puritans—Fiction. 2. New England—Social life and customs—
Colonial period, ca. 1600–1775—Fiction. 3. Diaries—Fiction.]
I. Title. II. Series.
PZ7.D8694Sar 1996
[Fic]—dc20   95-39249

February 1, 1651

Father says to practice my letters this night, so I shall write here. Dear Elizabeth visited this morning. We worked on our embroidery and dipped the last of the candles. Elizabeth was less merry than is usual for her. She worries for Roger. He is studying himself to near illness, she says, but must have his Greek and Latin perfect by Examination Day. Of all Elizabeth's brothers, Roger is closest to her, always good-hearted. He did look tired last Sabbath and I pray he will not exhaust himself studying. He smiled and spoke with me after meeting again.

Mistress Goddard came calling last eve with Mistress Weldon and Goodman Tiller. She is polite to me in Father's presence, but I see her little frowns when he is not looking. Only here on these secret pages can I admit how little I like her. I can barely stand it when she pats my cheek or straightens my bonnet ties. It is good she has stopped keeping her dame school. The children are better for it.

I find I can write no more about Mistress Goddard. I miss my own mother so much. I am so afraid.

CHAPTER ONE

The meetinghouse smelled of lye soap and damp wool. The Tithingman passed, walking down the aisle with his knobbed stick held loosely, scanning the prayer benches. Sarah was trying to listen to Reverend Terrence's last sermon. It was so *cold*. She rubbed her palms together.

Sarah waited until the Tithingman had gone by, then shifted on the hard oak planks. Careful to keep her skirt and petticoats clear of her little iron foot stove, she stretched her legs, pointing her toes, then arched her back. Instantly, Sarah felt Mistress Goddard's glare from across the aisle.

Without meaning to, Sarah glanced sideways and met the older woman's eyes. Mistress Goddard shook her head disapprovingly and Sarah looked away quickly.

Sarah was almost thirteen and she knew she was old enough to sit quietly through the sermons. But she felt strangely restless this Sabbath. She was finding it difficult to pay attention.

Everyone sat hunched over, the men's leather hats pulled low over their ears. Sarah heard a dog growl, then whimper as it was quieted by its owner. A frown touched Reverend Terrence's thin lips as he spoke. There to warm their owners' feet, the dogs often got into fights that interrupted his sermons.

Shivering, Sarah buried her hands in her skirt. She wanted to turn slightly and look at Elizabeth, but she did not dare. Reverend Terrence's voice rose, then dropped to a whisper. When he paused, Sarah could hear the wind gust outside, battering the clapboard walls and the shingles on the roof. Overhead, the heavy oak beams held steady, unshaken. Sarah stared at them as Reverend Terrence began again, talking now about the sin of Pride. His voice was low, each word precise. When he paused once more, the wind had dropped.

Sarah heard the unhappy lowing of an ox on the commons pasture. Or maybe it was Nan or Brownie, tethered at the rails outside. Sarah stretched out her legs again and drew another sharp look from Mistress Goddard.

Sarah pretended not to notice and looked sidelong at her father, sitting beside her. His spine was straight, his eyes fixed on the pulpit. His hands were in his lap, the callouses on his palms stained dark from the forge.

Sarah leaned forward just enough to see her father's face. He was lost in Reverend Terrence's sermon and hadn't noticed her squirming. Mistress Goddard would tell him later, of course. She never missed a chance to criticize or correct.

Mistress Goddard was very pious and very strict. That was why so many of the town's children had been sent to her dame school to learn the ABC's and to read their Bibles. Sarah had. So had Elizabeth and her brothers. Sarah knew her father thought Mistress Goddard would make a wonderful stepmother for her. Sarah shivered again and moved her feet closer to her foot stove.

Reverend Terrence's breath hung in the air like smoke as he read a passage from the Bible. Sarah stole another glance at Mistress Goddard.

Her posture was rigid, erect, and her white bonnet was pulled tight to cover her graying auburn hair. Her Sabbath clothes were perfect. Her blouse and skirt were homespun linen, plain, deep brown. Her doublet laces were tied primly, beneath an apron and neckcloth of immaculate white. She was childless and a recent widow. Sarah knew she should feel sorry for her, but she didn't. Mistress Goddard never seemed sad or lonely—and she certainly never had much sympathy for anyone else.

Sarah rubbed her hands together again. Her own mother had died nearly four years before of a fever that had taken dozens of lives in the town. Her father was sad and lonely. And he was going to marry Mistress Goddard, if she would have him. And she just might, Sarah thought. Her father made a good living shoeing oxen and horses in the summer and making clay bowls and pots in winter. He was honest and good and even handsome. Sarah sighed. Maybe Mistress Goddard would choose someone else. Every widower in town was chopping her kindling and carrying water for her.

Sarah counted to fifty, then shifted again on the plank bench. She risked a quick look off to her left, where Elizabeth Ludden sat with her family. Elizabeth, as she often did, met Sarah's gaze as though she had felt the look like a touch. Her eyes twinkled. Then, with an almost invisible tilt of her chin, Elizabeth gestured toward the aisle and Sarah knew the Tithingman was coming back.

Sarah fastened her attention on the pulpit. Reverend Terrence was still preaching his sermon, but all she could hear were the quiet footsteps of the Tithingman. Goodman Harrick was tall and broad shouldered, but he could move like a cat when his job as Tithingman required it. Had he seen her squirming? Looking at Elizabeth? The footsteps approached, then stopped, just behind her. Out of the corner of her eye she could see the Tithingman extending his stick.

Her heart racing, Sarah held her breath, then realized it wasn't the knobbed end of the stick this time. The Tithingman wasn't about to poke her for being restless. He had reversed his grip on the smooth wood and was reaching past her.

Sarah watched the dangling foxtail as it swung from the stick, nearing old Master Hatham, in the pew in front of her. He was sound asleep, leaning against his ample wife, his head on her shoulder. The Tithingman lowered the fox-tail just far enough to brush the end of Master Hatham's nose. The old man started, jerking back into wakefulness. He straightened up, without looking right or left, and his wife pretended not to notice anything as the Tithingman moved on.

Sarah watched Master Hatham sit stiffly, his white hair rumpled where he had leaned on his wife's shoulder. He was very proud and Sarah knew he had to be terribly embarrassed. It was hard for anyone to stay awake through an entire day of sermons, especially after noon dinner, the Sabbath House meal of cod and pottage and hasty pudding or samp with honey. Sometimes Sarah had trouble staying awake, too, especially in the summer when it was hot. Now, with the wind pounding at the doors, there were enough drafts to keep her alert.

But I am still not attending to the sermon as I should, Sarah thought, feeling guilty. She fingered the ties of her bonnet, then smoothed her heavy wool skirt. It had been dyed with logwood and iris, but its blue-lavender color was fading with every washing. Without moving her head or shifting her posture, Sarah glanced again at Elizabeth, whose deep-yellow skirt and fitted white blouse of smooth English cotton shone against the dark, well-cut coats and trousers of her father and six elder brothers. The four youngest boys still sat in the boys' pew, with others their age. Elizabeth's mother was in somber colors, too, her clothing stylish and well made. Blond Elizabeth looked like a pretty songbird among crows.

The thought made Sarah smile and she ducked her head to conceal it. What was wrong with her this Sabbath? Reverend Terrence usually held her attention. She liked his powerful voice and the blaze of his dark eyes. Elizabeth thought him handsome.

Sarah blushed and ducked her head again, afraid Mistress Goddard would look across the aisle at just the right moment and see the pink spreading across her cheeks. Sarah closed her eyes for a moment and prayed. What were all these improper thoughts? She felt so odd, like something was fluttering inside her, trying to get free.

A sudden sharp banging from the pulpit startled her. Reverend Terrence had lifted the hourglass, then set it down without turning it over. The sermon was finished. He was looking out over the pews as he always did to see how his words had affected the townspeople. Sarah heard her father's gentle exhalation and knew he'd been rapt, caught up entirely. She felt her cheeks burn once more. When Mistress Goddard asked her what she had learned from the closing sermon she would have nothing to say. Then would come the piercing, accusing look Sarah remembered all too well from her days in Mistress Goddard's dame school. All school mistresses were strict. Mistress Goddard's birch rod had never been far out of reach.

Sarah's father gently touched her shoulder. He was standing, turning toward the rear of the church as they began the first hymn. Her yellow skirt swirling, Elizabeth managed to catch Sarah's eye. She made another tiny motion with her chin, this time toward the doors. Her mouth silently formed two familiar words. "Walk home?" Then she flashed a smile, so quickly there and gone that Sarah caught her breath. What if someone saw? Elizabeth arched her brows, waiting for an answer.

Sarah nodded once, a tiny motion. Satisfied, Elizabeth faced the back and waited for her mother to open their hymnal.

Sarah couldn't see the Tithingman without turning. He was probably nudging the youngest Callant brothers in the boys' pew. They usually got unruly toward the end of Sabbath meeting. Sarah glanced at her father. He hadn't seen Elizabeth's smile. Sarah was glad. Her father already thought Elizabeth too bold, too careless in her manners.

Sarah sang the hymns as well as she could,

keeping her tuneless voice soft. It had been Mistress Goddard who'd taught both her and Elizabeth to sing quietly since neither could sing well. Sarah remembered Elizabeth crying, heart-broken at seven years old because Mistress Goddard had shushed her until the hymn was a bare whisper leaving her lips.

Sarah's father's voice boomed forth, sure and true. He looked young, almost happy. At home, in the evenings, he often looked tired. Sarah knew he was lonely. Most men his age had a wife and at least six or eight children. He needed more than one quiet daughter to fill his heart and his house. Maybe it would be good if he married Mistress Goddard. She was an excellent cook and everyone admired her hard work and her piety. Her husband had died nearly a year before. Few women waited more than six months. She would marry someone soon.

The last hymn soared to a close, voices thickening the air around Sarah; then it faded. People began to stretch, talking quietly as they pulled on mittens and gathered their children.

Sarah's father's eyes were dark and peaceful from the long day in church. He looked across the aisle. Sarah followed his gaze and saw Mistress Goddard smile slightly, her hands fussing over her bonnet and blouse. Sarah spoke quickly. "May I walk with Elizabeth?"

Her father's eyes came back to hers. "I can see no harm in it."

Mistress Goddard took a step toward them. Sarah heard the older woman's voice in response to her father's, but the meetinghouse had gotten noisy and she couldn't understand what they were saying. Her father bent to close the draft vents on the foot stove so the coals would die, then he straightened. He moved into the aisle. Mistress Goddard was suddenly there, whisking him away, her somber skirts brushing Sarah's.

Sarah watched them go. Mistress Goddard was paying more and more attention to her father. For the last three Sabbath evenings she had come visiting with friends to discuss the sermons and pray. They would marry. And it was going to be awful.

Sarah forced the thought away and tightened the ties on her dark leather doublet, then pulled her good linsey-woolsey jacket closer around her shoulders. The cloth was coarse, but Sarah loved it. It wasn't as itchy as the rough flax threads in her everyday dark-brown fustian coat.

Sarah turned to see Elizabeth staring questioningly at her. She nodded and Elizabeth smiled a tiny smile, then looked away. Her brother Roger was whispering something in her ear. Sarah watched them.

She always felt shy and clumsy around Elizabeth's brothers. Especially Roger. He was a scholar, learning Greek and Latin, and holding his own in discussions with Reverend Terrence and the other ministers. He would go to Cambridge College. He was handsome, too, in a dark, thoughtful way.

As Sarah walked toward them, Roger frowned. "You will want more coat than that for walking home."

Before she could say a word, he was shrugging out of his heavy English wool jacket and was lifting it for her to slip her arms into the sleeves. Sarah blushed at his attentions. Since Roger was almost sixteen and a good deal bigger than she, the coat fit loosely, even over her own thick, homespun jacket.

"Thank you," Sarah said, wishing she could think of something more clever.

Roger smiled. "Pray send it back with Elizabeth?"

"Of course," Sarah assured him, feeling the extra warmth seep into her skin. "You are very kind."

Roger smiled again, distracted by something

his father was saying. Then Elizabeth pulled at Sarah's hand and led her down the aisle between the pews to the heavy plank doors, which had been flung wide on their leather hinges. People from the back pews were already outside, talking quietly, getting ready to go home. The Callant boys walked with their parents, so much alike in looks that it was hard to tell them apart. The eldest was a good scholar, but as much of a troublemaker as the rest.

Sarah paused beside the doors. A notice of a pig and freshened milk cow for sale fluttered in the wind next to an announcement of an upcoming marriage, and a badly printed sign on rough paper that advertised the need for a wood joiner's apprentice. Elizabeth nudged her.

As they stepped outside, Sarah caught her breath. The wind had dropped and a patch of western sky had cleared. The late slanting sun glittered across the snow. The pillories and the whipping post threw long shadows, almost black where the footprints in the snow were deepest. There were not yet candles flickering behind the oiled-paper windows of the log Sabbath House, but in an hour or two there would be.

Inside the Sabbath House, Sarah knew, weary families would be packing up for the long ride homeward. Or, if the storm closed in again, some might stay the night at friends' homes, choosing to travel on the morrow, without threat of darkness overtaking their plodding oxen. Their animals would be well sheltered if they decided to stay. The far end of the Sabbath House was a stable, built for just such a purpose.

Sarah took a deep breath of the icy clean air, then stepped outside, pulling Roger's coat up around her chin. She led the way down the wide stone steps.

"At last," Elizabeth whispered from behind her, "we are released."

Sarah blushed. Elizabeth's boldness sometimes made her uncomfortable. But she nodded, understanding perfectly. She felt as though she were stepping free from a stale-aired prison. It was wrong to feel so, but she did.

Pausing on the trampled snow in front of the meetinghouse, Sarah looked back. A new wolf's head had been nailed to the weathered wood, shot for bounty. The deep-gold eyes were almost closed, their wildness stilled forever.

"I wish," Mistress Goddard said from behind her, "that they could kill them all."

CHAPTER TWO

"You will not tarry or wander?" Sarah's father asked, his breath a cloud as he spoke. Mistress Goddard was beside him, waiting. All around them, people were talking somberly, quietly, leading horses or maneuvering sleds toward the road. Sarah was trying hard to be polite, respectful. She wasn't feeling respectful. All she could think about was how much she hoped Mistress Goddard would marry someone other than her father. Sarah tried to erase the thought. It was absolutely improper.

She listened as Elizabeth's parents chatted politely with her father and Mistress Goddard for a moment, then started down the path, surrounded by Elizabeth's brothers. Roger looked back at Sarah for an instant and smiled. Then he turned and leaned to hear something his mother was saying as they walked toward the tying rails where their horses were tethered.

Sarah stared at the trampled snow. A few deep ringlike tracks stood out among the blurred impressions made by leather boot heels. Elizabeth's mother had worn pattens strapped to her shoes to keep them above the dirty snow. Sarah pointed at the tracks and whispered, "Lynn shoes?"

Elizabeth nodded without speaking, her eyes almost apologetic. Sarah glanced down at her own heavy, scuffed leather shoes, then watched the flow of people emerging from the meetinghouse. Quiet and orderly, the last families were moving out onto the trodden paths that crisscrossed the commons in every direction. Many wore plain leather shoes like her own. Only a few had comfortable, stylish footwear.

Shoes made in the town of Lynn were as fashionable and well made as any from London. They were, of course, expensive, but Elizabeth's father owned three fishing boats and was building another.

He could well afford such shoes for his wife.

"Be careful walking, and mind the Sabbath, Sarah."

Her father's voice made her instantly ashamed. Fancy shoes hardly mattered to the piety of her soul. Whatever made her think about them on the Sabbath? Sarah could feel Mistress Goddard looking at her intently, but she refused to meet the older woman's eyes. She nodded and her father smiled at her.

Elizabeth was standing quietly, her eyes down and her face composed. She was always withdrawn around Mistress Goddard. But most children were, especially anyone who had been to Mistress Goddard's school. They all remembered her fury at interruptions, outbursts, or anything she saw as laziness. Poor Thomas Kinder had worn a dunce sign around his neck all winter. Hope Winslow had spent half her days on the one-legged stool, uncomfortable, because she bit her fingernails and stammered. Sarah sighed. Why couldn't her father see Mistress Goddard's unkindness?

Waiting for him to tell her she could go, she looked up at her father. "Discuss the lessons in the sermons," he instructed her.

Sarah nodded. She and Elizabeth always talked about what had been said from the pulpit. Everyone did. But sometimes Elizabeth disagreed with Reverend Terrence. Sarah knew she should tell her father. But then he would probably never let her see Elizabeth again. "Good girl," her father added absently, patting Sarah's head as he turned away, listening to something Mistress Goddard was saying.

Sarah watched her father escort Mistress Goddard toward the heavy wooden sled pulled by Nan and Brownie. The oxen stood patiently, their massive heads close together as they huddled against the freezing air. Elizabeth nudged Sarah, then started off across the commons pasture. Sarah followed.

There were dozens of paths on the commons, worn by people and livestock across the wide snowy meadow. The meetinghouse and the Sabbath House bordered the north end of the commons. The town's oldest buildings were on the south edge. The three old wattle-and-daub structures that had been built by the Fullins family still stood, but no one lived in them now. They were used as barns, divided up into stalls and pens inside. The Fullinses' eldest son had built one of the largest new houses along the road into town. Elizabeth's family lived near his, in a two-story house with little triangular windows of real glass.

Elizabeth walked slowly, lifting her yellow skirt daintily. It was only then that Sarah realized that she, too, was wearing pattens, wobbling along on the ungainly metal rings that held her shoes clear of the snow and frozen mud. Elizabeth had been too kind to even show her the new, expensive shoes. Sarah chided herself. Her envy of Elizabeth's worldly wealth was a sin. It was God's blessing that Elizabeth's father and brothers were doing so well, that codfish were so plentiful.

Sarah said a silent prayer of thanks as she walked. There were many blessings to count. There had been no starvation this winter, thank God. The year before had been awful, and the year before that even worse, with some families near death after the turkey corn and barley crops had failed. After months of trying to rid the fields of the flocks of grain-stealing passenger pigeons, the townspeople had survived the winter by eating the pigeons themselves. Almost no one ate them now—the taste of pigeon reminded everyone of that terrible time.

Sarah shuddered, thinking about the famine winter, the way her father had gotten thinner and thinner, the gray, strained pallor of his skin as he went out each morning to check his snares and bird traps. And yet he had remained quietly hopeful, his strength keeping her from the black terror that clenched at her painfully empty belly.

Sarah inhaled the sharp scent of wood

smoke, rising from every chimney in town. For now, at least, there was enough to eat, and no sickness. Elizabeth glanced back at her and frowned. "Something is worrying you."

Sarah smiled. Elizabeth always seemed to sense her thoughts. "I am still afraid sometimes. But this year the harvest was plentiful."

Elizabeth dropped back to walk beside her. "And my father says we will never fish even a twentieth part of the cod from the seas. In every evening prayer he gives thanks that his parents left England."

Sarah didn't answer immediately. Sometimes she wished her grandparents had *stayed* in England. They had been wealthy there, but had lost everything going first to Holland, then coming here. They had spent their fortune finding a place to practice their Puritanism without fear. If they had stayed in London . . . Sarah knew her whole life would have been very different.

Elizabeth was watching her face. "You imagine yourself going to London balls in grand gowns, don't you?"

Sarah was unable to suppress a tiny laugh. "Perhaps. But it's terrible now. I should be grateful I am not there."

Elizabeth nodded solemnly. "A fish merchant told my father that he shall never go back. This last year they had dead lying in the streets from the sickness."

Sarah had heard such stories. She had prayed that they were not true at first. But too many people had brought the same bleak news.

"My father says there is plague all over France and Spain." Elizabeth's voice was small, timid. By the end of her sentence she was almost whispering. Sarah nodded without answering. Some people said it was foolish to import anything from England now, that the sickness could hide in cloth, or even in unspun wool.

Sarah looked at Elizabeth's English wool coat, then realized that Roger's coat was imported, too. She touched the thick, dark-gray cloth. She had never worried about it before; her father had no money to buy English linen or wool.

Elizabeth tripped. Sarah caught at her arm. "It's these pattens," Elizabeth said, "I am going to take them off."

As Elizabeth bent to undo the straps that crisscrossed over the tops of her shoes, Sarah really looked at them for the first time. The shiny dark leather was obviously supple and soft.

"Are thee injured, child?" an elderly voice inquired.

Sarah looked up to see Goodwives Farner and Temple approaching them. Their neckcloths were tucked into heavy fustian coats and their bonnets were pulled close, framing their wrinkled cheeks. Elizabeth raised her head and saw them. "I am well, thank you," she answered politely. "I am only taking these off before I pitch headlong into a snowbank."

Both women smiled at Elizabeth as she bent over again, her blond curls escaping from beneath her bonnet. They paused on the path and Sarah smiled at them. She liked them both. Goodwife Farner was well known for her weaving. Her skirt and apron were made of heavy linen, the thread spun so evenly that the smooth cloth hung perfectly.

Goody Temple was less neatly dressed, but her clothing was clean and she smelled of the herbs she grew and hung in her kitchen to dry. The beds of fragrant lavender and precious wolf's bane, rosemary, and comfrey near her house were kept free of stones and weeded carefully all summer long. All of her fourteen children were grown up. All eight of her daughters were good gardeners.

Elizabeth straightened up. She warmly thanked the two older women for their concern. Then, pattens dangling from her right hand, she began to walk again. Sarah followed. Without the hindrance of Elizabeth's pattens, they quickly outdistanced the elder women, who walked slowly, chatting in low voices.

"I think my father is going to marry Mistress Goddard," Sarah said once they were alone again.

Elizabeth wrinkled her nose and stopped. She turned and tugged Roger's coat up higher around Sarah's neck. "If your father does marry her, do you think she will allow our friendship? I fear she will not. She disapproves of my family, and of me."

Sarah did not answer. She had been worried about the same thing for a long time. It was entirely possible that Mistress Goddard would forbid her to see Elizabeth once she could. And her father would likely go along with it.

"My father is so strict," Sarah said finally, unable to confess her fear more directly.

"And mine is not," Elizabeth admitted. "My father almost settled in Rhode Island. He would have, except for the excellence of the ship builders here."

Sarah still didn't trust herself to answer. In Rhode Island the ministers had fewer rules and less control over people's lives. Sometimes she wondered what it would be like to live there.

"I think the ways of Rhode Island are better than here," Elizabeth said, lifting her chin defiantly.

It made Sarah uneasy when Elizabeth began talking like this. It was dangerous. Sarah half turned, scanning the paths around them for eavesdroppers. No one was close enough to hear.

"I apologize," Elizabeth said quickly. "I will try to be more seemly in my speech."

Sarah looked into her friend's eyes, grateful to end the subject. "My father is so strict," she said again.

Elizabeth kicked lightly at the snow. "And Mistress Goddard even more so."

Sarah walked a little faster. She did not want to think about what her life would be like if her father married Mistress Goddard.

Elizabeth took the next path that led south, and they walked on, following the edge of the pasture, past the tanner's house, inhaling the awful smell of the leather soaking in its stagnant brew of acorns and foul water.

"Better than in summer," Elizabeth said, holding her nose with two delicate fingers. Sarah grimaced in agreement, pinching her own nostrils closed. In summertime she could barely stand to walk this way at all. The rotten, bitter stench was strong enough on a hot day to make her eyes water. She felt sorry for the Barrent children, having to live near the tanning ponds, and having a father whose hands and clothes were always stained black-brown, who always smelled of curing hides.

"He's only afraid of spoiling you," Elizabeth

said. It took Sarah a moment to realize what Elizabeth was talking about.

"My father?"

Elizabeth nodded. "He only wants to make sure you are pious, and that you marry well. You are his only child, after all." Elizabeth made a face. "You cannot imagine how *I* envy that." Sarah watched Elizabeth tuck a stray blond curl back under her bonnet. "It must be so quiet and pleasant without brothers."

They had talked about it many times. Elizabeth loved her brothers, but they teased and tormented her. Her father doted on her, but her mother expected her to help with all of the household work and there was a great deal of it.

Sarah knew that Elizabeth got tired of cleaning, cooking, mending, spinning, soap-making, candle dipping, and all the rest. She did, too. Her father was proud of her housework—but for the two of them, there wasn't that much. He still did a little of the sweeping and cleaning as he had when she was small, even though she was old enough to do everything. For Elizabeth, the chores were endless.

"Your father is probably courting Mistress Goddard because he'd rather not be alone when you marry," Elizabeth said quietly, half turning and slowing her step. "You're nearly thirteen now,

Sarah. It won't be but a few more years at most."

Sarah stepped over a little drift of snow that crossed the path. When she thought about marrying, her thoughts always drifted to Roger. She trusted Elizabeth with nearly all the secrets of her heart, but she had never told her this one. What if Elizabeth said something to Roger? What if he didn't really like her and was only nice to her because she was Elizabeth's friend?

Sarah stayed quiet, hoping that Elizabeth would change the subject. Lately, she had been talking about marriage more and more often. But then, half the young men noticed her more than was proper. Elizabeth was very pretty.

"Will Roger begin at Cambridge College soon?" Sarah asked to break the long silence. Elizabeth stopped, smiling at her. Sarah looked aside, wondering if Elizabeth could tell how she felt about Roger. She glanced around to keep from meeting Elizabeth's gaze.

Goody Farner and Goody Temple, absorbed in talk, were still walking slowly, well back on the path. All across the commons, scattered groups of people walked quietly, silhouetted against the stark whiteness of the snow. Because it was Sabbath, no one was speaking loudly or laughing. The children were held tightly, especially those young enough to distract their elder siblings from the sober conversations about the sermons. The Tithingman and the Watchman would be alert all day, making sure Sabbath rules weren't broken.

Elizabeth cleared her throat. "If you did marry Roger, nothing could please me more." She reached out and touched Sarah's hand.

Sarah felt herself blushing. She began walking, concentrating on the squeaking of her heavy leather shoes against the fresh snow. She heard Elizabeth's breathing quicken as they started uphill, leaving the commons, heading past the three old wattle-and-daub stables that had been the Fullins family homes. The truth was that Roger was unlikely to settle for the daughter of a blacksmith and she knew it. He was going to be a scholar, a minister, a prominent man. For an instant, she pictured Roger, Elizabeth, and herself walking toward Mistress Goddard's, six years before, little children trudging through the snow.

"We are all growing up," Sarah said, looking determinedly at the path before her.

"My older brothers will all be apprenticed or on the ships soon, except Roger," Elizabeth said from behind her.

The foul smell of the tanner's had faded with distance. The air now held an odor of fresh cut wood from the cooper's yard. Half-finished barrels stood against the plank fence. Piles of curved wood staves showed from beneath a dusting of snow. The cooper hadn't brought them in when he should have and now they would have to stay out until after Sabbath sundown.

Sarah and Elizabeth were passing between Whitmant's log stable and a stubbled field of turkey corn now. The few remaining stalks were darkened by weather and cold.

Sarah's stomach felt tight, uneasy. "We should discuss the sermons." She glanced at Elizabeth, then hesitated. She hadn't listened to the afternoon sermons at all and the morning service seemed dim and distant. She couldn't think of a single thing to say.

Elizabeth pointed ahead to a narrow curving path that led toward the woods. "Let's take the old Indian Road. Please? The snow is so pretty in the woods."

Sarah shook her head automatically.

"Sarah." Elizabeth's voice was soft, pleading. "There's no harm in it."

Sarah couldn't argue. People—especially the children, looking for firewood as they went back and forth to their work weeding the turkey-corn fields—used the path every day in summer. The only reason it was less used in winter was its steepness. Sarah looked down into the trees. She had always loved the old path. Some of the trees grew in high, forced arches, cut back by generations of Indians using the path to travel from the forest to the salt marshes where they gathered clams and fished.

Elizabeth's eyes were intense, earnest. "I promise to talk about the sermons."

Sarah hesitated, examining Elizabeth's eager face. She glanced back up the wide, well-worn path they were on. There were several groups of older boys walking some distance behind them. Goody Farner and her friend had disappeared, probably on their way to visit someone who lived on this side of the commons. Behind the boys, the Beenes family made their way homeward, going slowly, both parents burdened by the weight of children too small to walk.

Elizabeth tugged at her sleeve and Sarah lowered her head, giving in. She led the way onto the Indian Road, placing her feet awkwardly in the untracked snow.

CHAPTER THREE

Sarah walked slowly. This part of the Indian Road dropped steadily, following the curve of the little valley that marked the end of the town proper. The oldest houses surrounded the commons, with fields and pastures just beyond, toward the river.

Sarah's grandfather had built one of the oldest thatched-roof clapboards, but after he died her grandmother had sold it to a whitesmith and bought passage back to England. Sarah remembered her, a small woman who rarely smiled. She'd had six children, but only Sarah's father still lived in the town. Sarah's two aunts had died when her mother had, when the fever had swept through the town. Her three uncles were all sailors, gone a year or two at a time, back only long enough to tell tales for an evening or two when they visited.

Sarah walked a little faster, picking her way down the path. The fever that had taken her mother had killed Reverend Terrence's two eldest children and Elizabeth's tiny sister—and so many others. Sarah's stiff leather shoes slipped a little and she caught her balance, wrenched from her gloomy thoughts.

The bark of the trees looked dark and impossibly wrinkled against the flawless white of the snow. It wasn't deep, except where the wind had drifted it across the path. Behind her, Elizabeth was walking carefully, her eyes on the ground.

Sarah searched her mind for some fragment of the sermons upon which she could comment. Then she spoke over her shoulder to Elizabeth. "Reverend Terrence believes that the sickness in England is God's judgment."

Elizabeth didn't answer immediately. Distant, vague voices from the town road above the woods drifted into the trees. "Reverend Terrence also thinks Anne Hutchinson was punished by God," she said quietly after a moment. She leaned close to whisper. "And you know, as everyone does, that it was the Indians who killed her."

Sarah shook her head, a little angry. "I must keep my promise to my father."

Elizabeth's face softened. "I apologize. Roger admires Mistress Hutchinson's rebellion. My father does as well."

"But she was claiming to know as much as the ministers," Sarah said, repeating what she had heard her father say many times. She stopped to face Elizabeth. "She thought *she* could interpret the Bible."

Elizabeth did not stop, but stepped briskly around Sarah. "Perhaps she *could*," she said as she passed, so softly that Sarah could barely hear the terrifying words.

Sarah's heart quickened. The dark trees had closed in behind them, the commons entirely hidden from sight now. The distant voices had faded. They were alone. Sarah started after Elizabeth, whose bright yellow skirt swung in flounces as she walked, pattens dangling from one hand, clinking in rhythm with her steps.

Sarah started to warn Elizabeth against getting her shoes wet, but didn't. Elizabeth cared far less for a pair of soft leather shoes from Lynn than Sarah would have. Sarah bit at her lip. For Elizabeth, there would never be missed suppers, whippings, or any other punishment for her opinions about Mistress Hutchinson's arguments with the ministers. And there would be more beautiful shoes. Sarah began walking faster, following Elizabeth on the narrow path.

"Do you know what I think?" Elizabeth whispered, spinning around. She jabbed at the air, her eyes flashing angrily. "The ministers knew that Anne Hutchinson was with child when they made her leave. Everyone knew it. She wasn't young. I think they wanted her to die."

Sarah stood still, her skin prickling. Elizabeth had barely raised her voice above a whisper, but the words still seemed to echo around them. Sarah's mouth went dry. Her father would punish her severely if he found out she had listened to such talk.

Elizabeth had tilted her head, lifting her chin. Her bonnet was pushed back and her eyes were glinting dangerously. Sarah finally lowered her eyes. "I am only trying to keep my promise to my father."

"We are," Elizabeth said quickly. "Reverend Terrence talked about Mistress Hutchinson this afternoon." Sarah couldn't hide her surprise. Elizabeth nodded knowingly. "Ah. Now I understand. You did not listen." Sarah ducked her head, flushing.

Elizabeth suddenly reached out and tapped her shoulder. "Naughty. If Mistress Goddard finds out, it will be a high stool in the corner for you. And no supper."

Sarah tried to smile at the joke. "If we do not hurry, Elizabeth, your father will send your brothers looking for us."

Elizabeth shrugged. "They'd not find us too quickly here, would they?"

Sarah turned involuntarily. Their tracks had marred the smooth snow, winding back away from them through the trees. No one else had used the path since the last storm. She stood uncertainly, the restless feeling that had been with her since morning rising inside her.

"Come, then," Elizabeth said quickly, her voice apologetic again. "I do not mean to upset you, Sarah. Come." She reached out to tug at the sleeve of the borrowed coat. "Roger is the cleverest of all my brothers," Elizabeth said quietly. She studied Sarah's face for a moment. "And he thinks that Anne Hutchinson was right to try to understand the sermons as she did. He even thinks it unjust to keep men who don't belong to the church from voting."

Sarah didn't answer. Roger had never told her that. It frightened her when Elizabeth said things like this. People who disagreed with the ministers ended up in trouble. If they weren't actually cast out into the wilderness like Anne Hutchinson had been, they were left out of town life, whispered about until they mended their errors or left on their own. Sarah imagined Roger being questioned by angry ministers. Elizabeth had begun walking again. Sarah hurried to catch up.

The path curved around a dense stand of bare trees, spangled with ice. The snow had deepened. Reddish willow saplings were slanted beneath the drifted weight. Gray-barked branches reached across the path above their heads.

"Oh, look, Sarah." Elizabeth stopped suddenly and pointed. "See it?" Her voice was soft and excited. A startled fox ran from them, its silent feet stirring the powdery snow. It leapt a fallen log, graceful, its body flowing like auburn flame up the hill. When it had disappeared, Elizabeth clenched her fist in the air. "If my brothers were here, someone would have a new hat."

Sarah smiled. "Then I am glad they are not." Her breath hung in steamy wisps around her face for an instant. It was getting colder. She looked up through the trees. The sky had deepened. Dusk was not far away. "We should hurry, Elizabeth."

Elizabeth frowned. "If your father gets angry . . . ," she began, but Sarah raised one hand, halting her in midsentence. Her father would not get angry if they got home before dark. Elizabeth led off. Sarah started down the slope, wondering if Elizabeth's parents ever really got angry at her. She knew they punished Elizabeth's brothers, but only rarely. Did they know what Roger said about the ministers? If Roger were *her* father's son, such talk would never be tolerated, or forgiven.

Sarah's mother had been kind, with a lilting voice and long soft hair. Her father had been happier when her mother was alive. Happier and less strict.

Elizabeth stopped abruptly again, pointing at a songbird high in a birch tree. Sarah frowned at her. "We don't have time." Elizabeth shrugged apologetically and walked on.

The woods got thicker as they went, the pine trees rising from the soft snow, their dark branches sighing quietly with every shift of the air. Everything was hushed. Sarah's footsteps, even her breathing, seemed muffled, lost in the snow and trees. She felt giddy, as though the path were endless. As they walked, she imagined it getting longer. Perhaps they would never reach the other end where it came out of the woods. They could just walk on and on through the soft cold silence, alone, without anyone to tell them to do their chores, to hurry to Sabbath meeting, to practice their writing or their Bible reading. Sarah shivered. Foolish thoughts.

Elizabeth was ahead of her, walking slowly uphill. She topped a rise and cried out. Sarah looked up just in time to see her pitch forward, then disappear. Sarah ran ponderously in the snow, frightened until she could see over the crest of the hill. Elizabeth was on the ground, fighting her skirts, trying to stand up, snow caked on her bonnet and face.

"Are you hurt?" Sarah floundered toward her friend. Elizabeth shoved her pattens into her pocket and managed to stand. She took a determined step downhill. Then another. On her third step, she slipped again, sitting down hard. She giggled, then covered her mouth, her eyes wide, drawing in a deep breath. "The ground beneath the snow," she said unevenly, "feels like ice."

Sarah brushed past her, walking carefully. "It's better here." An instant later, Sarah's right foot skated wildly and she fell, sliding sideways down the steep path. She bumped to a stop against a fallen log and couldn't help laughing. The ground was as slick as river ice.

Once she managed to stand up, Sarah felt herself flush. What were they doing? Sliding in the snow was forbidden on any day, and this was Sabbath. Her skirts were heavy, powdered with snow. She shook them out, looking uphill at Elizabeth.

"My shoes," Elizabeth said slowly, carefully setting down her right foot, "are going to be wet through. There's snow down inside now." Sarah's cheeks stung as the cold air prickled at her blush.

Elizabeth smiled a little, jerking her coat straight, slapping at her sleeves. Then she smoothed her yellow skirt with both hands. "There." Elizabeth began to walk.

On her third step, Elizabeth's foot arced upward as though she were trying to kick something and she landed hard on her back, sliding downhill toward Sarah. Sarah had time to take a quick breath before Elizabeth thudded into her knees, gasping with helpless laughter.

Sarah bent forward as Elizabeth clambered upward, clutching at her. For a few seconds they half stood, supporting each other. Then Elizabeth waltzed Sarah in a small circle, stepped free, and immediately sat down, sliding again, her feet sticking awkwardly out in front of her, her head thrown back, grinning. Near the bottom of the slope, she began to roll, over and over, her arms loose, giggling helplessly, coming to a stop against a snowdrift that crossed the path. She lay still, her grin fixed and her eyes closed.

Sarah felt her heart constrict. Frightened, trembling, she made her way down the hill, skidding wildly, her feet so far apart that she had to pump huge circles with her arms to keep from falling. She faced sideways, slowing just as she reached Elizabeth and managed to stop herself by sitting down.

Elizabeth snapped her eyes open and looked up at Sarah, her bonnet slightly askew. She laughed aloud. Sarah felt mirth tickling at her. "You trickster!" She laughed, then bit her lip. It was Sabbath. "We should . . . you must stand up," she whispered and Elizabeth nodded.

Sarah stood, braced her feet as well as she could, and extended her hand. Elizabeth took it. They both began to slide, still standing, holding each other. When they collapsed onto their knees, they were both laughing hard.

Sarah closed her eyes, biting hard at the inside of her cheek. But the laughter wouldn't die. She felt weak, silly, like a baby. All she needed was a baby's puddin pillow tied around her middle to soften her falls. Waiting until her breathing steadied, she stared at the dark trees. Then she stood up again, more slowly this time.

After a moment, Elizabeth stood, her face pink and beaded with melting snow. Her eyes were shining, her lips trembling, and Sarah knew she was still fighting laughter, too. Sarah felt her own laughter tickling at her throat. To calm herself, she looked up the path, which disappeared around a curve in the distance.

Without warning, Elizabeth began to giggle softly. Before Sarah could even understand what she was doing, Elizabeth had turned away from her and was struggling back uphill, climbing the ice-slick incline by walking to one side of the path and using the leafless willow stems to pull herself upward. Her yellow skirt clung to her legs, the hem white with snow, wet patches showing darker where the snow was melting.

At the top, Elizabeth turned and opened her arms like a disheveled bird. Sliding, graceful at first, then flapping her arms like a sea gull tumbling in a windstorm, she slid toward Sarah. Her laughter bounded through the dark trees, merry, and her eyes were flashing. Sarah grinned, watching her. Their eyes met as Elizabeth got closer, her arms spread wide. They were staring at each other when Elizabeth slammed into Sarah and they both fell, laughing.

Flushed and breathing hard, Sarah disentangled herself, pulling her skirt free of Elizabeth's, and staggered to her feet. She took a shaky step backward and looked up the hill. The restless feeling that had been with her all day seemed to swell and blossom inside her body. "My turn," she whispered. Elizabeth's muffled giggles followed her up the hill. The cold air pricked at her cheeks, the giddy laughter was still finding its way past her lips. Her legs, as though they belonged to someone else, hauled her upward, her hands reached for each low branch, each clump of willow twigs.

At last, Sarah turned, laughing aloud, bobbing as her feet skated crazily on the frozen ground. She slid a little ways, lifting her eyes to look at Elizabeth. They both giggled aloud as Sarah righted herself, just managing to stay upright.

Sarah pretended to dance and Elizabeth exploded into laughter, both hands over her mouth, her eyes shining. Sarah let herself slide a few feet, her arms out, looking past Elizabeth at the beautiful, snow-heavy trees. Suddenly, Sarah's laughter faltered, then collapsed. She fought to keep her balance, staring.

Just visible near the curve in the path, a dark figure stood watching. Sarah gestured helplessly and Elizabeth turned. In the instant before the figure disappeared back around the curve, Sarah fought an urge to cry out.

"Mistress Goddard," Elizabeth whispered into the silence.

Sarah could not speak. Her laughter was a frozen weight, heavy and painful inside her chest.

CHAPTER FOUR

For a few moments, Sarah stood still, unable to move. Then she started down the path. She fell twice, heavily, woodenly. At the bottom, Elizabeth reached out, her face filled with pain. "I will say it was my fault," she whispered.

Sarah pulled in a deep breath, then let it out. Nothing felt real. The woods were too quiet. "I think she only saw me," she whispered. "Perhaps she will only tell them that much."

Elizabeth looked up the path. "You know how much she dislikes me, and my family."

Sarah could find no answer. It was true. But

why had Mistress Goddard been walking the old Indian Road? Had she heard them laughing and come looking? Sarah's eyes ached and she wished she could cry. Mistress Goddard took such satisfaction in discovering anyone's wrongdoing. She would be nearly running up the road with the news.

Elizabeth patted Sarah's shoulder. "Maybe she didn't recognize us. She was quite far away."

Sarah felt hope flutter in her heart, then the wings stilled. "We knew *her*."

"Your father will be so angry." Elizabeth looked up at Sarah. Her eyes were intense. "God will forgive us. I believe that. We have broken Sabbath, but He forgives us. Even if no one else does."

Sarah shrugged, unable to find comfort in Elizabeth's words. She had sinned. They both had. Perhaps God did forgive them. But Reverend Terrence would not, nor would her father.

"They could make us go to the pillory," Elizabeth breathed, her fear showing suddenly in her eyes.

Sarah shuddered, imagining it. She had seen the punishments all her life, but she had never thought it could happen to her. She looked into Elizabeth's pale face. Twice she began to speak, then stopped. Nothing she could say was going to change anything. They had broken the Sabbath. In her case, there would be two punishments. One from the town ministers and one from her father. She realized suddenly that the woods were darkening.

"We have to go now," Elizabeth said, reading her thought. "I would give anything if I had not led you astray."

Sarah reached out to touch her friend's cheek. "You did not."

Elizabeth shook her head. "I did. I began it. I went back up the hill and . . ."

"There you are!"

The sudden shout whirled Sarah around, nearly tripping over her skirt. Roger was coming toward them, arms out, plunging down the path. He paused, pushed his hair back from his eyes and smiled at them. "This should have saved time, not made you later," he called. "Is anything amiss?"

Sarah could read the uncertainty on Elizabeth's face. Normally she confided in Roger. But this time it was different. Sarah shook her head, the kind of tiny motion they used to communicate at dinner when no talking was allowed, or in the meetinghouse. Roger could not help them. Telling him would only upset him. Besides, everyone would know soon enough.

"Elizabeth?" Roger said as he half walked, half skated down the last part of the icy incline. "Has anything happened?"

Elizabeth pressed the back of her hand against her lips, then slowly lowered it. "I . . . fell. That's all. I am not hurt."

Roger looked gravely at Sarah. "And you?" he asked. "Are you safe?"

Sarah could not meet his eyes. "Yes."

Roger tilted his head, taking in the trodden snow, the reddish stems they had broken climbing back up. Sarah stood silent as he looked at their wet skirts, their snow-caked jacket sleeves.

"I saw you turn off," he said finally, setting his feet carefully. "But then we got home before you, so I went back." He looked uneasily past Elizabeth and his eyes focused on Sarah. She swallowed.

"What is the matter?" Roger asked.

"Nothing," Elizabeth said quickly. Too quickly.

Roger examined her face. He looked puzzled, but when he spoke he asked no more questions. "It will soon be dark and Mother will want your help at supper."

Sarah watched Elizabeth nod, her face pale now, all the twinkling laughter gone from her eyes. Roger was studying his sister, too. Sarah brushed at some snow on her hip and pushed back her bonnet. The wet wool itched her fore-head. She cleared her throat, meaning to speak, but nothing would come out. She gestured instead, pointing down the path.

Roger started out slowly, sliding with every step. "The ice is terrible," he said over his shoulder. Elizabeth made a soft answer that Sarah couldn't hear as she started after him, her shoulders hunched. Sarah followed her, trying to find tiny hillocks and hollows to better her footing. It was hard. As they rounded the curve and started up the last incline, Sarah saw the set of hurried tracks Mistress Goddard had left in the snow. If Roger saw them, too, he said nothing, and she was grateful.

It was not nearly as slick once they started up out of the woods. It was getting dusky, the shadows of the trees seeping like dark water across the snow. Sarah's feet moved without thought. She could not cry, or even pity herself. Everyone knew the rules of the Sabbath. Every master, mistress, goodman, goodwife, every child. The cooper had a horse that he boasted would not allow itself to be ridden on the Sabbath. Even an animal seemed to have more piety and more sense than she did.

Sarah's thoughts seemed slow, separate, and she examined each one the way a baby looked at acorns in a gathering basket: Her father would be shamed. He would be furious. Mistress Goddard would gloat over Elizabeth's punishment. Her father might forbid her to see her truest friend ever again.

Sarah missed her footing and fell onto one knee. She felt the sting of the freezing snow through her soaked stockings. As she struggled with her wet skirt, Roger looked back and saw her making her way back onto her feet. She waved so he would know that she was not hurt.

"Not much farther," he called to her. He scuffed at the powdery snow that had fallen the night before. Elizabeth, her face a mask of misery, turned and tried to smile.

Sarah shook out her snow-soaked skirt once more, the cold and wet seeping into her skin, into her heart. Her ankles ached above her shoe tops and her toes burned with cold. She pulled Roger's coat closer around her throat. He would want it back in a moment.

Roger stepped onto the town road first, then Elizabeth. Sarah followed, weighted by her fear and dread, as if her feelings had tangled around her feet, slowing her steps.

"I suppose we must just . . . go home," Elizabeth said, looking into Sarah's eyes, then to the left, toward town and the lane that led to her father's house.

Sarah tugged at the sleeve of Roger's coat,

working it down over her arm. "You will want this," she said quietly. Roger started to protest, but she pulled the other sleeve free, shrugging out of the coat. "I thank you, Roger," she said politely. "I am sorry that I got it wet."

Roger leaned to take the coat and his hair fell forward onto his forehead. He pushed it back. "I'm only pleased I found you safe."

Elizabeth came close and leaned to whisper in Sarah's ear. "I am so sorry, dear Sarah."

"It is not your fault," Sarah said. Roger was frowning curiously. She wished desperately that he was not there, that they could talk. But what, really, was there to say? For a few more seconds they just stared at each other.

Roger was waiting. "We will walk with you."

"No," Sarah said. "There is too little time."

Elizabeth forced a smile. "I'll visit after morning work." Sarah couldn't respond. They both knew there would be no visit.

It was obvious Roger could tell something was wrong, but he remained silent as Elizabeth reached out to touch Sarah's hands. Sarah looked up at the sky. Night was falling. The darkness would soon be complete, pressing itself against the snow, against her skin.

CHAPTER FIVE

Sarah walked stiffly toward home. The road was tracked with fresh sled ruts and deep heart-shaped oxen tracks; the countryside families had already passed on their way home. She felt the icy air needling through her damp clothing. She had gotten used to the extra warmth from Roger's heavy coat.

As Sarah rounded the first curve in the road, she could hear the cutler's children singing hymns and see the mild glow of tallow candles behind Master Parry's papered windows. Tall pines surrounded the steep-roofed house, ink black against the deep-gray sky. Hearth smoke scented the air and Sarah's mouth watered at the smell of roasting venison. The hymn ended and a prayer began, Master Parry's booming voice leading the children's.

There was always noise from Master Parry's house. He had fourteen children and kept several dogs; there was also the racket of his work. On the morrow the usual cutler's din of hammering and grinding would begin again. Planting and harvesting tools always needed sharpening and resteeling in winter.

Sarah kept walking. She was chilled through, but somehow it seemed unimportant. Priscilla, Goodman Bishop's eldest daughter, was outside her father's house when Sarah passed. Her arms full of firewood, Priscilla paused and stared into the darkness. Any other evening, Sarah would have greeted her and stilled her curiosity. Priscilla was pious and good-hearted, always ready to help with spring cleaning or soapmaking, singing to lighten the work. They had been friends all of their lives. What would Priscilla think of her now?

Sarah's feet were like stone, senseless with cold. She rounded the last bend, then came to an uncertain stop, staring at the little square house she had been born in, the house her mother had died in. The darkness was nearly complete. Her father would be angry and worried.

A sled team and a saddle horse were tethered to the crooked fir tree that grew beside the house. Sarah bit at her lip. Mistress Goddard and her friends were inside. Her father must already know.

Before Sarah could make herself move, the door opened and her father came out, his face lit by the smoking tallow candle he held. He squinted, peering into the night. Sarah found herself walking toward him, drawn by the friendly flicker of flame. Her shoes scuffed against the cobblestone walk.

"Sarah?" His voice was hard.

"Yes."

"What has caused such delay on the Sabbath?"

As she stepped onto the stone threshold, he came closer and tilted her chin upward. "Pray answer, Daughter."

Sarah cleared her throat, looking past him. Mistress Goddard and Goodman Tiller sat on the hearth bench, talking. Mistress Weldon stood near the fire, her face somber. She looked exhausted. Her husband had been hurt raising a beam and she had had to do much of his weaving, as well as all her own work, since the accident.

Her father touched her cheek, then stepped back. "Come in, Sarah. Warm yourself."

Sarah, confused by his kindness, followed him into the keeping room. He shut the door behind them and dropped the bar. The guests began speaking again, in low, serious voices. Mistress Goddard gestured, making some point. Sarah bent to pull off her shoes and woolen stockings. Without speaking, her father crossed the room to hang her wet stockings on the drying pegs beside the hearth. He took down her dry pair and brought them back to her, searching her face.

"You walked home alone." It was not a question.

Before she could speak, her father went on.

"We looked for you. Mistress Goddard heard voices and walked a little way down the old Indian Road. . . ." He paused and Sarah could only wait, lowering her eyes, her heart pounding. Her father cleared his throat. His voice lost some of its edge. "Elizabeth is apparently not a proper companion for you. Nor her brother Roger. Mistress Goddard saw them in the woods." He paused and patted her shoulder. "I am glad that you left them. But you should have come directly home."

Sarah drew in a quick breath, trying to

understand what he had said. "Father, I . . ."

He held up a hand to hush her. "Put these on. You'll catch an ill."

Sarah bent to pull on the dry stockings. When she stood straight again, her father touched her cheek, looking into her eyes. "Change your wet skirt now. I will make tea. Then we will talk about this. Go," he ordered when she hesitated. "You are nearly frozen."

Sarah's teeth began to chatter, as though her body only realized how cold it was once her father had spoken. She glanced longingly at the hearth as he handed her a candle tray. She awkwardly gathered her skirt with cold-stiffened fingers and went down the narrow hall, her stockinged feet silent on the smooth plank floor. Behind her, the conversation went on. The low voices faded as she closed the door of her room.

Inside, Sarah stood for a second, staring at her narrow cot, at the rosebuds she had so carefully embroidered on her linen bedcover. Elizabeth had helped, had taught her the whip-stitch she had used on the stems.

What had Mistress Goddard told her father? She hadn't even seen Roger, had she? Had she hidden and watched them after they thought she was gone?

Sarah set the candle tray on the little table beside her bed. Elizabeth was her best friend, the one person in the world who never scolded or condemned her for anything, who always listened. And Sarah knew her father was almost certainly going to forbid their friendship. He had said it . . . Elizabeth was not a proper companion. Nor Roger. Sarah's throat tightened painfully. Roger.

Trembling, Sarah took her second-best skirt from its peg. Then she hung it back up, uncertain. Her father might chide her for wearing her second-best while she was in disgrace. Or he might prefer that she show respect for the Tithingman by dressing decently in case he came this evening.

Sarah rubbed her hands together, bowing her head. She wanted to pray, but she could not. Sliding in the snow was a foolishness, a waste of time. It had always been forbidden and it always would be. To have done it on the Sabbath was beyond anyone's tolerance. She was fortunate that her father had not met her at the door with a willow rod. Perhaps he didn't want to embarrass himself further in front of his friends and so would say no more until they'd gone. Sarah shuddered. He must be so ashamed of her.

The sound of one of the oxen bawling in the shed behind the house startled her. How long had she been standing here? Sarah pulled her bonnet off, raking her hands through her tangled hair. The cloudy little mirror on the wall beside her mother's armoire showed the paleness of her face, even in the candlelight, and her dark eyes. They looked enormous, too big for her face.

Sarah pushed back wisps of her fine hair. Did Roger think she was pretty? He acted as if he did. She leaned close to the mirror, then pulled away, horrified at herself. She had broken the Sabbath and now she was giving in to the sin of Vanity. What was wrong with her? It hardly mattered what she looked like when her heart was so tarnished.

Sarah perched on the edge of her bed. The corn-husk mattress rustled. When she was little, she had imagined the rustling was the whispering of angels, watching to make sure she was good. Well, she had certainly not been so today. But why was it so wrong to play on the Sabbath? To laugh? Why was it forbidden to slide in the snow, to sled? Sarah stood, astonished at her thoughts. Shaking now, her hands unsteady, she looked back up at her clothes pegs. She untied her skirt's waist and let the sodden wool drop to the floor. Hesitating, then reaching out, she took down her everyday clothing. If the Tithingman came, he would find her dressed as though this were a normal evening.

"Sarah?"

Her father's voice pierced the plank door and she winced. "Yes?"

"Hurry yourself. Supper is late enough."

Sarah nodded, trying to still her trembling hands, then realized that he could not see her. "I will, sir," she said respectfully. She slipped her everyday skirt on over her still-damp petticoats and traded her wet doublet and blouse for the soft everyday blouse she had made out of an old petticoat from her mother's marriage chest.

Sarah smoothed her everyday skirt. She had always loved it. It was a deep brown, only a little faded now. The cloth was still strong and sturdy, even though it was stained with cooking and cleaning and the oil she rubbed into her father's tools to prevent rust. Sarah knotted the waist ties and pulled her everyday bonnet from its place. This one was grayish wool, and she liked it better than her Sabbath bonnet. It had been made from soft cloth Elizabeth's mother had given her, a scrap from a dress she had cut down for Elizabeth a few years before.

"Sarah?"

She jumped, startled that he was still there. She frantically stuffed the ends of her hair beneath her bonnet, then faced the closed door, squeezing her hands into fists to make them start warming up, gathering her courage. When she picked up the candle and opened her door, her father was no longer standing there.

Stamping her cold feet, Sarah walked back down the hall and into the keeping room. She set her candle into one of the sconces that hung on the wall and looked around for the little pewter snuffer. Unable to find it, she licked her fingers to pinch the wick. She burned herself a little and blew on her thumb.

Her father was poking up the fire. Sparks showered the back wall of the hearth. Sarah could picture them bursting from the chimney, each one a shining arc until the snow ended its life. Mistress Goddard and Goodman Tiller were still talking, their Bibles at hand. Mistress Weldon was leaning forward to listen. Sarah tried to hear what Mistress Goddard was saying over the crackling of the fire, but could not. Her father turned and saw her.

"I am very proud of you," he said quietly, once he was close. Confused, Sarah stared at him. He pulled her toward the fire, guiding her onto the hearth bench. "Warm yourself."

Sarah nodded politely at Mistress Weldon, who moved aside. She spread her fingers across the fire's heat, feeling the tiny stabs of pain that meant her flesh would soon be coming back to life. Her feet were just beginning to tingle. Why would her father be proud of her? Nothing made sense.

Her father was smiling at Goodman Tiller, who had asked a question Sarah hadn't heard. "The Tithingman will come for them soon," her father said after a little pause and there was satisfaction in his voice. "Mistress Goddard saw them clearly. In their fancy coats and shoes." There was disdain in his voice. He fingered his plain dark jacket, touched his somber hat.

Sarah's heart beat heavily. Understanding was seeping into her mind as slowly as warmth from the fire was entering her skin. The coat. Kind Roger's coat had fooled Mistress Goddard.

"Elizabeth and her brother will be punished." Her father's voice was heavy, final, and he looked down at her. "Mistress Goddard walked all that way to look out for you, while I drove the oxen back up the town road. She is most considerate of your well-being, Sarah."

Sarah looked up at her father. There was love

in his eyes. And something else. Pride. He truly thought she had left her companions to keep from joining in their sin.

"I must have missed you by a few minutes," he added, still looking at her intently. Sarah averted her eyes. The prickling in her thawing hands had gotten painful. Now it all fit together. Her father believed she had not sinned. Mistress Goddard *had* seen her—but Roger was going to be blamed for her wrong.

Sarah wanted to tell her father that it was an awful mistake, that she was the guilty one, not Roger. She wanted to plead with him to forgive Elizabeth, to explain that Elizabeth was bold, but that her boldness was not usually dangerous. It was beautiful, to be envied. But she could not speak. A lifetime of obedience weighed upon her tongue and closed her lips. And she did not have the courage to change the pride in her father's eyes to shame.

Sarah wrung her hands and regretted it instantly. Her chilled skin felt as though a thousand needles were poking at her. Her feet were beginning to ache as they warmed up. Her hip felt bruised from one of her falls, and her eyes stung, flooding with tears. The fire blurred, the merry amber sparkle changing to a slurry of gray and orange. The voices of the guests had stilled. Mistress Weldon stood a little way off, staring into the flames.

Sarah's father put his arm around her shoulder. "I know it is hard to see a friend do wrong. But I am grateful that you left them. What way did you take coming home? You must have gone all the way back to the commons."

Sarah tried again to speak, but before she could begin, Goodman Tiller was talking. "Reverend Terrence will be harsh with both of them, I fear."

Mistress Goddard made a sound of agreement and Mistress Weldon added her quiet assent. Sarah watched her father frown. His eyes were hard and angry now, the love well hidden again. "They were *playing*!" The last word was an outraged explosion. "They were sliding, playing in the snow when Mistress Goddard saw them. *Laughing*." He shook his head. "That family is too lenient. They are spoiled."

Suddenly Sarah's father was reaching down to take her hand. He pulled her to her feet, his face stiff with authority. "Prepare supper now, Sarah. Our guests are hungry and I think I can persuade them to join us."

He then began the intricately polite exchanges that led up to asking his guests to stay for the meal. Preoccupied, even Mistress Goddard stopped watching Sarah.

While her father was talking, Sarah stood still, unable to move or to speak the truth. Her father's words hung in the air around her, along with the quiet responses of Mistress Goddard and the others. But Sarah wasn't listening to anything but her own thoughts.

Roger was innocent of anything but kindness. And she was a coward.

CHAPTER SIX

"Sarah?" Sarah heard her father's impatience. It was probably the second or third time he had said her name. She looked up at him.

"Our guests have agreed to share our poor supper," he said. Sarah nodded, almost grateful to be told what to do. Supper. She had to fix supper now.

Her father and Goodman Tiller were bringing a second bench from its place near the wall. Together they placed it beside the dinner table, opposite the smaller bench Sarah's father usually used. Once it was in place, Mistress Goddard seated herself grandly. "And how is your husband?" she asked as Mistress Weldon sat down beside her.

Mistress Weldon's face clouded. "He is better some days, but his leg still hurts him." Mistress Goddard murmured her sympathy.

"Sarah."

Her father was frowning. Sarah picked up the biggest piggin and went to the water barrel. Was Elizabeth helping her mother make supper now? How soon would she be weeping, listening to a scathing lecture from the Tithingman? Elizabeth was bold, but she was fragile, too, and easily hurt. And what about Roger? Soon she would have to tell her father the truth.

For a moment Sarah imagined the Tithingman thumping the heavy door boards with his stick. Maybe the Watchman would come with him, holding his lantern high enough for all to see that there was trouble on this Sabbath.

Sarah had made supper a thousand times. Her hands went about their tasks as her thoughts tumbled from one awful image to another. First, she would boil water for the samp. She lifted the full piggin to the wooden hearth shelf, placing it far to one side, where her sleeve could not catch on the long handle-stave and spill the water. She reached up and took down the dipping gourd. Deftly, she slid it at an angle beneath the water's surface in the piggin, then raised the gourd full and dripping. With a little swoop of her wrist, she shook the droplets free, then carried it cleanly across the hearth to the small iron saucepot.

Sarah forced herself to think a moment. What would she prepare to go with the samp? Stewed venison would be easiest and quickest and her father liked it. She still had bread from last baking day and she could make apple betty for dessert. There was no time to build a fire in the stone oven inside the hearth; it took hours to heat up. The iron bake kettle would have to do.

Sarah set the saucepot, using the long handle to give it a final turn so that its slender iron legs were level and steady in the thick bed of coals. She placed the lid on it, then worked the bellows to brighten the fire.

The bellows had come from her father's shop out in the oxen shed. There was a tiny hole in one side so they no longer worked well enough for the forge. For cooking, though, they were better than most. Within just a few minutes, the fire was crackling, the coals angry red.

Sarah noticed her steaming stockings and shoes on the drying pegs and turned them over to heat the opposite side. Then she went back to her cooking. The voices of the adults rose and fell behind her. She knew they were talking about the sermons. Normally she would have tried to listen, but this Sabbath their words seemed too far away.

Sarah swung the arm of the pothook until the big iron kettle for the stew was over the flames. The iron lug bar her father had made in the forge creaked as she used the dipper gourd to fill the kettle with water. Sarah was grateful for the lug bar. She knew three girls with burn scars from kitchen work. Constant Helms had the worst. Her mother's lug bar of green wood had burned through unexpectedly; the heavy iron pots had crashed from the hearth, splashing boiling stew that soaked her thick woolen stockings. Sarah shivered. Tenderhearted Elizabeth had cried the first time Constant had shown them the yellow, puckered skin on her legs.

Outside, the ox bawled again. The wind had picked up. The oiled paper over the windows trembled and Sarah shivered, even though her skin was flushed now, heated by the hearth flames. She strained to listen to Mistress Goddard talking to the other adults.

". . . some severe punishment," Sarah heard the older woman say in her low, tight voice. "Of course, I was not told."

"They will do what is proper," Sarah's father said evenly. Mistress Goddard murmured an agreement. Mistress Weldon added something Sarah couldn't understand. She risked a quick look. Her father stood close to Mistress

Goddard, looking earnestly into her face.

"I very much appreciate your care and concern in this matter," he said warmly.

Mistress Goddard looked down modestly. "It is not my place, but I do so want little Sarah to . . ." Her voice dropped and Sarah couldn't hear the rest of the sentence. She strained to listen as she used the dipping gourd again, to finish filling the big kettle. It was obvious that Mistress Goddard was trying to convince her father that she would be a good stepmother. Sarah shuddered. Mistress Goddard could never take her mother's place. Never.

Sarah pushed the arm of the pothook to center the kettle over the hottest part of the fire. Then she picked up a short candle in a pronged tin holder and used a strand of straw to carry a small flame from hearth to wick. Once the candle was lit, Sarah raised it carefully and walked to the back wall of the keeping room. She opened the narrow door that led to the cold room and the root cellar. Before she went in, she took down a basket from the shelf above the door and turned back to steal another glance at her father and Mistress Goddard.

They had settled on the bench near the door. Their privacy was obviously more important than warmth or comfort. They were both frowning, their faces troubled and austere as they spoke. Sarah watched her father for a few seconds, then pushed the door open and went into the cold room. She pulled the door closed behind herself to keep the little bit of warmth in the house from escaping.

A string of frozen sausages was draped over a willow rod alongside two hanging, frost-white turkey carcasses; a haunch of beef swung, rock hard, from an iron hook. These were barter goods for her father's work. Farmers often came leading a team of oxen to be shod. Most carried a saddle sack filled with fresh meat or apples or corn. Her father went to outlying farms to shoe horses, but the oxen were too heavy to stand on three hooves while he worked on the fourth. They had to be shod standing, supported in a special sling her father had built in the shed.

Sarah bent to lift the root cellar trapdoor, latching it back with the wooden hook on the wall behind. Then she went carefully down the stone steps her father had set into the raw earth. Holding her candle out in front of her, she ducked under the support timber and into the cellar. The candle made a golden globe of light and a crowd of flickering shadows on the roughly timbered walls.

Sarah reached to untie a bundle of dried

pumpkin that had been threaded onto a flax string. She slid five large pieces down the string and set them in her basket. Then she tied and rehung the bundle. The candle flickered and Sarah closed her eyes, trying to think only of dinner. She had squash. Now she needed meat.

The salt barrel had a whittled wooden spike tied to a leather loop fastened to its side. Sarah used it to spear a goodly portion of the dark, preserved venison, lifting it slowly to lay it in her basket. She replaced the spike. Then she turned to the corn bins.

It had been a good summer. The bins were full of fat, dried corn kernels that had been shelled off the cobs, and dried beans, plump and dusty. They had a barrel of fine meal and two barrels of ground samp—corn that Goodman Tobb's wife had cracked, in trade for the repair of an iron bake oven. Sarah turned and took a gourd from a rack beside the entry door. She filled it with samp and added it to the meat and the wrinkled slices of dried pumpkin in the basket. Apples next.

Sarah paused for a second, closing her eyes again. She leaned unconsciously toward the stairs, putting all of her strength into listening. What were they saying while she was gone? Sarah could not hear her father's voice or Mistress Goddard's. She tilted her head to listen.

"Sarah!"

Her father's voice was so close that Sarah jumped. She went to the foot of the stone steps, her heart thudding. He was standing at the top, holding an oil lantern in one outstretched hand, peering down at her.

"Sarah?"

"Yes." Sarah could hear how upset she sounded, how tired. She took a deep breath. It was time to tell her father what she had done. If she waited until the Tithingman came, it would be worse.

"Mistress Goddard sent me to make sure you had not fallen or had some accident," her father said. The lantern lit his face strangely; the light deepened his eyes and his cheeks seemed more hollow than usual. "Answer me, Sarah. Have you?"

Sarah hid her irritation. Mistress Goddard was certainly acting the part of concerned step-mother-to-be. "No," she managed. "I have not." Her voice sounded muted, forced. Her father did not seem to notice. "You do not have too much to carry?" She shook her head. She pulled in another deep breath and straightened her spine, trying to find a word to begin with, a word with enough courage to pull all the others behind it. But before she could speak, her father straightened up. Then he was gone, the glow of the lantern throwing his shadow from one wall to the other as he turned, fading as he went back through the cold-room door.

Sarah's candle flickered again, and she looked at it, her eyes stinging. Why hadn't she spoken? The candle sputtered. It would gutter soon. The wire frame of the save-all would keep the wick from collapsing for a few minutes, but after that, the pool of tallow would snuff out the flame and she would be alone in the dark.

"Apples," Sarah whispered the word. For an instant, she couldn't make sense of anything. The word *apples* sounded like nonsense. With stiff fingers she went through the apple box and found eight sound fruit, big ones, only a little shriveled. She put them in the basket along with three sweet potatoes, parsnips, and a few limp carrots from last summer's garden. Then she carefully picked up the candleholder.

The low flame had melted the tallow into a bulging puddle and the pewter holder felt hot in her fingers. Taking care to hold it level, she slipped her left arm beneath the leather loops that served as the basket handle and lifted it carefully. Then she went up the stone steps, her feet as heavy as her heart.

CHAPTER SEVEN

Sarah's father was standing near the fire, gesturing to emphasize something he was saying. Mistress Goddard was sitting on the bench close to the hearth again. She nodded politely as Sarah entered; Sarah managed to nod back. Goodman Tiller and Mistress Weldon sat at the dinner table still, talking quietly, a Bible open before them.

The basket felt clumsy swinging from Sarah's arm as she crossed the keeping room, passing close to Mistress Goddard on her way to the hearth. Mistress Goddard sat impossibly straight, a smile shaping her thin, stern lips. For an instant

Sarah imagined shouting at her to leave. The impulse left her ashamed. She fumbled for a place to set the basket.

"Sarah, do you need help?" Mistress Goddard asked, misinterpreting. Sarah shook her head.

"She is quite a good cook, truly," her father told Mistress Goddard. "Her mother taught her when she was young and Elizabeth's mother has spent time instructing her since."

"That family," Mistress Goddard said softly, "has more to learn than to teach."

Sarah stared into the flames for a few seconds. Her father was never going to let her see Elizabeth again. Not once he knew what they had done. And he was going to marry Mistress Goddard.

Goodman Tiller's voice rose a little. He was reading the Bible aloud now. Sarah's thoughts flickered to Roger, with his gentleness and his deep-brown eyes and his independent ideas. She knew her father would never let her marry a man who argued with the ministers. Sarah took the poker from its hook and stirred the fire a little, watching the sparks shoot upward.

Over the soft voices behind her, Sarah heard the water boiling in the saucepot. She reached for the dipper gourd, then used one of her father's clay bowls to mix the corn samp with cold water. She pushed the thick mixture from the bowl into the boiling pot, stirring out the lumps with a wooden spoon. Then she added a pinch of salt and replaced the lid.

Using a pot rag to protect her hand, she pulled the saucepot's long handle to reposition it farther from the huge flaming logs at the back of the hearth. Sarah realized the voices behind her had fallen silent and she thought she could feel Mistress Goddard's critical eyes on her back. The pot bobbled a little and the water inside hissed as it sloshed up onto the hot iron. Sarah deliberately loosened her grip on the handle and took a slow breath. She started over, working the handle back and forth, carefully resettling the iron legs in the deep bed of coals, where the samp would simmer without scorching.

Half listening as the discussion behind her shifted from one topic to another, Sarah cut the meat into small pieces and dropped them into the kettle, then began to dice the squash. She used a wooden trencher to cut upon, sparing the knife the dulling it would have gotten from the stone hearth.

Sarah's thoughts would not remain with the work her hands were doing. Had the Tithingman already come for Elizabeth? Or the Watchman? That would be worse. Master Barton was unbendingly strict.

Mistress Weldon raised her voice. "A sailor

told Goodman Tobbs, who told Master Chandler, who told me, that half of London is sick and dying."

"It is the work of God," Mistress Goddard said evenly.

"I've heard this news, too," Sarah's father put in. "The sailor said children are dying. Babies. All of London is like a great hospital."

Sarah continued cutting squash from the basket, dropping the pieces into the stew simmering in the kettle. Hot water splashed her wrist and she flinched, waiting for Mistress Goddard's response.

"It is all God's work," came the even voice again.

"Well," Sarah heard her father murmur. "It just seems such a terrible thing. Little babes."

Sarah, moving with slow, precise carefulness, concentrated on her chopping. How strange it was to hear the gentle warmth in her father's voice even when he was obviously disturbed by Mistress Goddard's reaction to the London sickness. He was courting her, of that there was no doubt.

Then Goodman Tiller spoke up. "London is a sinful place."

The conversation began again, with Mistress Weldon agreeing. Sarah tried to follow the conversation but found she couldn't. Her own heart was too loud, and her thoughts kept leaping to Elizabeth and Roger.

Sarah lifted the lid of the corn samp and stirred it vigorously. It was thickening a little too soon. She added water from the piggin and stirred. Glancing at the stew, Sarah reached above her head and broke off a few sprigs of dried thyme from the hanging bundle. The herb garden had been her mother's great treasure. Sarah tended it carefully in the summer and saved seed every fall. She wanted, someday, to buy seed from England or France. Her mother had raised flowers, too. The house and the woods around it were decorated every spring with tansy, chamomile, live-forever, and larkspur—wildlings from her mother's flower beds. Sarah's eyes stung, and she squeezed them shut for a second.

She had not cried over her mother in a long time. Her mother was with God, in a happier place than this one by far. Sarah stilled her shaking hands against her thighs, hoping her father wouldn't notice her sudden tears. Or Mistress Goddard.

Once the sharp empty feeling had eased, Sarah bent to the woodbox and pulled out a stout green log. With practiced grace, she hoisted it up and over the pots, letting it drop onto the burning wood at the back of the hearth. It landed perfectly between the heavy iron firedogs. Sparks exploded up the chimney.

Mistress Weldon began talking about her son's upcoming marriage to the cobbler's middle daughter. Then they all returned to discussing the day's sermons. Sarah peeled and cored the apples, mixed honey and a little of her precious lard with dried bread crumbs, and layered them in the bake-kettle. She raked a space clear of ashes and set the bake-kettle in it, then used the hearth rake again, this time to bury the kettle in glowing coals.

The stew was done. Sarah faced her father, waiting until he noticed her. "I beg your pardon," she said politely. "Supper is almost ready."

Mistress Goddard stood. Sarah crossed to the high shelf and took linen napkins and spoons down. Placing them on the table, she blushed and avoided her father's glances when she accidently let one spoon fall, banging on the wood. Then she pulled the four clean trenchers from the middle, glad that they had enough; *she* could use the one she had cut squash on.

She set the clean trenchers around the table, unsure whether Mistress Goddard would sit beside her father this time, as her mother would have done, or on the other side of the table as was proper for a guest. There were only two benches at the table tonight and the way her father and Goodman Tiller had placed them, there was really no choice. Mistress Goddard caught her eye and nodded approvingly as she set the place beside her father's. Sarah pretended not to notice.

The noggins stood in a row on a wide shelf above the wood box. Sarah brought them down and filled the small wooden mugs, one by one, from the cider cask. Then she set a full noggin by each trencher.

Sarah stirred the stew once more, making sure it was well cooked. Then she placed the bread slices in a toasting fork to warm over the fire. A moment later, her father and Mistress Goddard were sitting at one end of the table on the bench her father and her mother had once shared. Goodman Tiller sat on the other bench with Mistress Weldon. Sarah laid knives at every place, then porringers for the stew.

Working quickly, Sarah poured the stew into a clay bowl and set a ladle in it. She placed this near her father. Then, she brought the warmed bread, wrapped in a clean napkin. She carried the samp to the table, setting the hot iron pot on a trivet to keep it from burning the table. At last, she went to stand by the sideboard near the hearth and bowed her head.

Mistress Goddard sat with her hands in her lap, her eyes down, until Sarah's father finished saying the meal prayer. Sarah stood quietly at her place until the adults began eating. Then she served herself quickly and modestly and went back to stand at her sideboard.

Sneaking quick glances at the adults, Sarah ate without tasting the food. When she saw Mistress Goddard looking across the room, she followed her gaze. Near the far wall stood Sarah's spinning wheel and her baskets of carded wool and spindle-wound yarn. She was a little ahead in her spinning this month. That was one thing Mistress Goddard would not be able to find fault with. She was an excellent spinner.

"Sarah has done a lovely sampler." Sarah looked up when her father raised his voice. "It has a Bible verse, and an ABC," he added, smiling. He nodded at her and she stared at him blankly. Mistress Goddard had an expectant expression on her face. Mistress Weldon and Goodman Tiller had stopped talking.

Her father's smile thinned and he cleared his throat. "Fetch the sampler to show Mistress Goddard." He spoke slowly and clearly, as though she were a little child of two or three, just coming into understanding.

Sarah nodded reluctantly, stepping away from her sideboard. She picked up the candle-holder she had carried to the cellar and crossed the room to get another. Her candle box. It was half empty; it was time to refill it from the box in the cold room. She lit the new candle from one burning in a wall sconce.

Sarah walked down the hall, scuffing her feet along the planks, carrying the candle well in front of her to light the way. Once in her room, she set it down, then sat heavily on the side of her bed. She knew what her father was doing. He was trying to show Mistress Goddard that she was a good girl and would be an accomplished young woman who would only be a credit to any woman who married him—in spite of the fact that her friends were frivolous Sabbath breakers. Mistress Goddard would hardly approve of her once she knew the truth.

Sarah forced herself back to her feet. If she were gone too long, her father would come looking for her. She reached to the top drawer of her armoire, another of her mother's wedding gifts. She pulled out her sampler. The needle was still in it; she hadn't yet finished the last of the climbing rose that went around the cross-stitched border.

Sarah started back down the hallway, walking as slowly as she could, the sampler dangling from her free hand. How much longer could she pretend nothing was wrong? How was she going to tell her father what she had done? Sarah stopped, caught by a sudden thought. Maybe, if she was upset enough about the Sabbath breaking, Mistress Goddard wouldn't marry her father.

"Sarah?"

Sarah walked quickly into the keeping room. Her father motioned her closer and took the sampler from her. Mistress Goddard made a great show of cleaning her hands on her napkin before she touched it.

Sarah went to her place at the sideboard and stood miserably, waiting for Mistress Goddard to say something about the stitches being a little uneven. They *were* uneven. Her needlework was not nearly as perfect as Priscilla's or Elizabeth's. Mistress Goddard examined the stitches for so long that Sarah began to fiddle with her food, pushing chunks of meat and squash around with her spoon. Then she remembered the apple betty.

Sarah turned just as Mistress Goddard looked up from her sampler. "I can see your hard work in this."

Sarah nodded without answering and went

to the hearth. Hard work. Well, it wasn't exactly the same as saying it was pretty, or fine. Mistress Goddard had found a way to criticize her and to sound polite about it all the while.

Mistress Weldon took the sampler and held it up so the firelight shone against the linen cloth. "It's very nice, Sarah. Beautiful roses."

"She spins well, too," Sarah's father added. "She always meets her due."

Sarah forced a smile for Mistress Weldon. Then she pushed the lifting stick beneath the bake-kettle's handle. Carefully, she slid the heavy kettle toward herself. Tipping the lid so that the coals and ashes spilled harmlessly to one side, she turned her head to escape the quick burst of fragrant steam. She peered into the kettle, tilting it toward the fire for light.

The apple betty was done, golden brown on top. Sarah exhaled, relieved. Mistress Goddard could find no fault with this. Nor could her father. Sarah carried the bake kettle to the table and set it on a second trivet. She went back to the hearth for a big wooden spoon.

"Ah," her father said. "Sarah has thought to prepare a sweet for us."

Sarah kept her eyes modestly down, waiting for Mistress Goddard to speak, but she did not.

Perhaps, Sarah thought, if there were nothing to criticize, she didn't bother to say anything. Sarah blushed at her disrespectful thought and averted her face, hoping her father had not seen her frown.

"Sarah, it is a very good meal," Goodman Tiller said. Sarah looked up to acknowledge his praise. She smiled a little, but he had already turned his attention back to the food.

Sarah returned to the sideboard and stood silently. No one was talking now. Sarah was too nervous to eat and this was an uncommonly large supper anyway. She and her father often ate only hasty pudding from their porringers in the evenings.

After a few minutes had passed, Mistress Goddard looked up from her trencher at Sarah, then at the others, one by one. Her eyes came back to Sarah. "Be sure to have the voider ready in case guests finish eating before the host," she said quietly.

Sarah set down her spoon and went obediently to the hearth where the voider basket rested on a shelf near the wall. They did not have a special voider for guests. This was the one they used every meal to gather up the soiled napkins and the meat bones and waste. It was clean, though. Sarah washed it every meal as her mother had taught her. Mistress Goddard should find it suitable enough. She picked it up and started toward the table.

"No, Sarah," Mistress Goddard said, stopping her midstep. "I meant only to have it ready. It is not proper to bring it yet."

Sarah saw her father nod, a tiny motion meant for her alone. Setting the basket down, she went back to the hearth. She could feel her cheeks warming with an angry flush. Had Mistress Goddard deliberately misled her, just to make her feel foolish?

In that instant, a loud banging on the door startled them all. Sarah stood paralyzed, her throat tight. There was no doubt who it was.

Sarah's father crossed the room and unbarred the door, opening it just a crack. A man's voice came from the other side. Sarah stared, unable to take her eyes off the door as her father opened it.

The Tithingman, tall, rough-faced Goodman Harrick, ducked under the lintel and stood solidly before her father.

"I apologize for the intrusion so soon after Sabbath sunset," he began, glancing into the keeping room. Sarah saw his expression change when he saw the guests. He had not noticed the horses tethered by the crooked fir.

"I have but a short message from Reverend Terrence," the Tithingman went on, his gaze falling on Sarah and sticking there, even while he spoke to her father. "Your daughter is to come to the meetinghouse in the morning, at first light. There's a matter to be decided and she will be needed."

Sarah's knees felt unsteady and she leaned on the sideboard. "Yes," her father said clearly. "Tell Reverend Terrence she will be there." Sarah watched her father close and bar the door. "Only tell the truth," he said gently. "Your friends will thank you for it one day." Mistress Goddard sat straighter on the bench and lifted her mug to take a sip of cider. Sarah forced herself to nod, her heart constricting. The truth was the last thing her father wanted to hear.

I am unsure of the date, but I suppose midnight has passed. I lie here, sick at heart. I should have told my father everything, but could not bring myself to speak in front of Mistress Goddard and the others. I will have to tell Father in the morning. He will feel tricked, angry that I let him believe in my innocence. But it will only be worse if he hears it first from Reverend Terrence.

I would give anything to talk to Elizabeth. And Roger. I am afraid of what Priscilla and Constant will think of me, of what everyone will think. My father will be so ashamed. I am. How could we have played like that? For a few moments it was as though nothing mattered, and of course that is folly. But it felt wonderful, too, and I wish . . .

Most of an hour has passed between the last line and this one. The candle is burning low and I can find no comfort in writing. This night feels as long and cold as a whole winter.

CHAPTER EIGHT

Sarah wasn't sure if she awakened, or if there was simply a time when she began to notice that the darkness was receding. She rose in the near dark and stood for a few seconds, staring at her closed door, then sank back down, and sat shivering on the edge of her bed.

Her diary lay beneath her pillow and she took it out, but could not see well enough to read what she had written the night before. The candleholder lay on the little table beside her quill pen. There was a stub left of the candle, but she would have to go to the hearth to light it. Sarah closed her diary and slipped it far beneath her cornhusk mattress.

Her father often had her copy Bible verses or write lists of her sins and mistakes in her diary. As far as she knew, he never read it, unless she showed him a certain page. But he might. She almost wished he would. It would be easier than telling him.

Sarah could see the amber outline of the narrow window high in the wall. It was getting light outside. She stood again, her bare feet cringing at the cold floor. The Tithingman had said first light. She had better hurry.

It was almost dark in her room, but it didn't matter. She knew where everything was. She pulled off her nightgown and cap and hung them on the highest peg on the right, where she always did.

Then, as she had the night before, Sarah hesitated. It made no sense to wear her everyday clothes to go to the meetinghouse. Yet her Sabbath outfit seemed wrong, too. Finally, she reached for her second-best clothes.

She pulled on her underclothes first and the pair of woolen stockings she had worn the night before, then she took down the skirt. She stepped into it and slipped it on over her hips, tying the waist with sleep-clumsy fingers. This skirt was russet brown, sturdy wool; it had belonged to her mother.

Sarah put on the blouse, tying the bodice closed. It was linen, of good quality. Elizabeth's mother had made it for her, cutting it down from one of her own English blouses. Sarah hurried into her doublet and laced it tightly for warmth, then impulsively took down her everyday bonnet, leaving the second-best on its hook.

Leaning close to the little mirror, Sarah ran her wooden comb through her hair. Impatient, she pulled hard at the tangles. Once the knots were gone, she gathered her hair and wound it around her hand, tucking the end through to make a loose bun. Then she pressed the soft grayish wool of the bonnet against her cheek for a moment before she put it on, careful to get every wisp of her hair beneath it.

Sarah stared into the murky mirror as she worked with her hair, but she really couldn't see anything in it. The room was too dark and the mirror was cloudy and scratched. Elizabeth's father had given it to her, a treasure she had never expected to own. The amazing thing was that her father had permitted her to keep it.

Once she was dressed, Sarah began to pray, as she always did. But this morning, her prayers were different. Instead of praying for strength against her sins, she prayed for the courage to face the ministers. She was frightened—so frightened that her breath was quick and light, like a cornered rabbit's. If Elizabeth was right, God already forgave them for breaking the Sabbath. That would not be true of Reverend Terrence. Sarah rubbed at her eyes, trying not to cry. She could not even pray properly. If only they had stayed on the town road.

"Sarah?"

She had been expecting her father's voice, but it still startled her a little. She stood quickly, staring at the sliver of lantern light beneath her door. "Yes, Father?"

"It is time to dress."

Sarah ran her fingers along the edge of the soft wool, where the bonnet touched her neck, nervously checking once more for stray wisps of hair. "I am," she heard herself say, too quietly. She lifted her chin. "I am dressed."

Outside the door she heard her father clear his throat. "Come, then."

Sarah slowly reached out and pushed the wooden handle.

"Are you hungry?" her father asked, holding the lantern higher to see her more clearly. He did not comment on her choice of clothing.

"No, thank you, sir." The idea of eating made Sarah feel sick.

"Then we shall only bank the fire and be sure of the coals before we go. I think we will not be gone overlong."

Sarah followed as he led the way into the keeping room. She crossed to the hearth while her father pulled on his coat and took down his hat. The woodbox needed filling. She would have to do it when they got back. There were two stout green logs left and a few sticks of dry wood.

Sarah put on the dry wood and worked the bellows to waken the sleeping coals back into flame. Once the dry wood was burning, she used the long-handled fire hook to pull the sticks apart. She didn't want them to burn too fast and suffocate the coal bed in light white ash before the green wood caught fire. She placed the fresh logs carefully, then stood back. She had only lost the fire once so far this winter. She did not want to go begging coals from a neighbor today.

"We must go," her father said from behind her. His voice was flat, even. Sarah got her coat down from the drying pegs, then her gloves, and, last, her shoes. The leather was stiff and brittle, uncomfortably tight as she took the first few steps toward the door. By the time she was on the snowy threshold, closing the door, the leather had begun to relax a little, pinching her less as she started toward the ox stable behind the house.

"No, Sarah. Come back." Her father said it in a lecturing tone of voice, as though she were a tiny child, running off in the wrong direction. "We will walk to remind ourselves of the virtues of Simplicity and Humility." He set off down the road, settling his hat down over his ears. Sarah followed. She would find a way to tell him before they got to the meetinghouse. She had to.

There had been no new snow during the night. Last evening's sled ruts and ox tracks had not filled in, but they had hardened, making the road slick and uneven. Sarah felt the cold seeping into her feet as she walked and wished she had worn a second pair of stockings.

The morning was gray and grim. The wind had died and Sarah was grateful. But it was piercingly cold, and the sky still seemed to press down upon the earth. The pines leaned close to the road, dark against the graying dome of the sky. Every household they passed was building up its morning cook fire, filling the air with wood smoke. She could hear Priscilla singing at her chores. The cutler's hammer rang out as they walked by. The road was deserted; this was a morning for staying home to work.

When they came to the edge of the commons, Sarah's father paused, looking across the wide meadow toward the meetinghouse. She tried to speak, but before she could even begin, he bent and kissed her forehead lightly, his eyes full of love and pride. Then he walked on and Sarah could only follow.

The meetinghouse looked bleak and weathered in the gray morning light. Beyond it, an untracked slope of snow lay white and perfect. Sarah found herself looking only at her father's back, his shoulders shifting with his long-legged stride, as they neared the doors. She could hear her heart thudding in her ears. She longed to hide her face in her father's dark coat, his strong arms tight around her shoulders, as she had done when she was little. But, of course, she could not.

They went up the stone steps. Sarah caught the toe of her shoe on the threshold, but her father took her arm, steadying her as he swung the door inward. Sarah thought for a confused and giddy moment that the meetinghouse was empty; then her eyes began to adjust to the dim interior.

The oil lamps burned in their wall sconces. A small candlewood torch had been set into the holder on the pulpit near where Reverend Terrence was standing. Beside him was a stocky, balding man. Sarah recognized Goodman Barton, the Watchman. His hourglass and lantern were set at his feet and his iron-gray brows were hunched and tense.

Reverend Terrence beckoned them closer. "Ah, good. We have not waited long."

Sarah met the Watchman's eyes for an instant as he looked at her, then she lowered her gaze. She had never really talked to him before. She had never had to. Reverend Terrence and her father exchanged polite greetings in somber voices.

"We are here, Sarah," Reverend Terrence said in a soft, careful voice, "to talk about your friends."

Now was the time to tell the truth, Sarah knew. Before Roger had to do it for her.

"They will be severely punished regardless of what you say," Reverend Terrence assured her, pausing for emphasis. "We shall make an example of them."

Sarah stared at Reverend Terrence, then at the Watchman when he cleared his throat. But it was her father who spoke next. "Tell them what happened, Sarah."

"Yes," Reverend Terrence encouraged her. His hawk's face tilted like a curious bird, he leaned toward her. When she did not answer quickly, he kept his voice kind and patient. "Tell us, Sarah."

Sarah looked above the men's heads, at the

oil lamp's smoky flame. An example. What did that mean? The pillory?

"Answer," her father commanded. "Tell them."

Sarah tried to imagine Goodman Barton smiling and could not. She blinked. What foolish thoughts to have now.

"Speak." Reverend Terrence's patience was thinning.

Sarah's throat had gone dry. All three men were waiting expectantly. Her father was beginning to look angry.

"Elizabeth and I . . . ," she began, then swallowed painfully. "Elizabeth and I walked . . ." She hesitated, her heart pounding.

"Yes?" Reverend Terrence prompted. His voice still sounded gentle, but his eyes were hard.

"We walked home on the old Indian Road," Sarah said, her voice thick and slow. "There was ice and . . ."

"Did Sarah's brother come with you?" Reverend Terrence interrupted her. His voice was even, controlled.

"Roger came when we were half the way home," Sarah answered. "But he . . ." She hesitated again. Then she lifted her chin. "Roger is very kind. He . . ."

"He is far too outspoken," Reverend

Terrence interrupted. "Disrespectful of authority."

Her father was staring at her. "Tell Reverend Terrence if you saw Roger break Sabbath."

Sarah wanted to speak. Her throat was so dry it hurt. She pulled in a deep breath, gathering her courage. "Roger did not break Sabbath," she said as loudly as she could. Her heart was like a drum against her ribs, pounding in her own ears.

Her father took her shoulders and turned her to face him. He was frowning fiercely. "Mistress Goddard saw him. And his sister."

"So she told Reverend Terrence," Sarah agreed, her voice almost a whisper. "But . . ."

"Mistress Goddard," her father said with slow precision, "was correct to do this."

Sarah shook her head; her father was not understanding her. It was so hard to talk. Her throat ached.

"I know that Elizabeth is your friend," he went on, "or so you have thought. Sarah, Mistress Goddard considers your welfare as tenderly as would your mother."

Sarah's heart ached. That was not true. It would never be true. "It was right to leave them," her father went on. "But it would have been best if you had then gone to him," he added, gesturing at Goodman Barton.

"Or to me," Reverend Terrence added.

Sarah watched her father nod. Then Reverend Terrence came closer, gazing into her eyes. "Each one of us has the duty to prevent sin, or to correct it."

Just then the meetinghouse doors swung open and Sarah recognized Elizabeth and her father, silhouetted against the glaring gray snow. Then, an instant later, the Tithingman and Roger stepped through the doorway. For a moment, they all stood just inside the door, still half-blind in the dim light.

When Elizabeth saw Sarah, she gave a little cry and, her arms open, started toward her. But her father stopped her, taking her hand to turn her around. He bent to whisper something in her ear. Elizabeth stiffened, but she did not struggle or speak. Instead, she stayed close to her father, staring bleakly at Sarah, her eyes flooded with tears.

Reverend Terrence tapped his fingers on the pulpit, making a hollow, disturbing sound in the awkward silence. Sarah felt her father's hand on her shoulder.

"Finish telling Reverend Terrence," he said, leaning close. Then he straightened. "Sarah will just tell her part," he said respectfully. "Then we will go home." Sarah heard the uneasiness in her father's voice and for the first time she realized that he was frightened, too.

"Yes," Reverend Terrence agreed. "Speak, Sarah."

Sarah drew a deep breath, afraid to look at Elizabeth for fear she would start weeping and be unable to talk. Her father squeezed her shoulder again and Sarah looked wildly from one stern face to the next. Abruptly her eyes fell on Roger. He was looking at her closely, concerned—for her, not for himself.

"Sarah!" Her father whispered insistently.

She licked her lips, desperate to speak, to end the awful pressure of her own silence, the pressure of her father's hand on her shoulder. "Elizabeth," she managed, then coughed. Her father was going to be so ashamed, so angry. She took a deep breath and began again. "Elizabeth and I walked the old Indian Road. And Roger . . ."

"I came upon them a little later," Roger interrupted, speaking clearly and loudly. "I followed to see that my sister and her friend were safe. I was acting foolishly. Sarah left us to walk home alone."

Sarah turned to stare at him. What was he saying?

Roger stepped forward. "After Sarah was

gone, I slipped and fell. I could not keep my feet and began to laugh. Then I began to play. It was very slick and I simply forgot the Sabbath and my duties. Elizabeth did nothing but watch me. If she laughed aloud, it was because I acted the fool and tempted her."

Sarah blinked, astonished. Roger was trying to take the blame for everything. He was trying to free both herself and Elizabeth from punishment. It was wrong. Sarah knew it was wrong. But deep inside her body a fear which had lain cold and heavy against her heart lifted a little. She knew she should speak. But her father's look of pride silenced her once more.

"You both broke the Sabbath?" Reverend Terrence asked, looking now at Elizabeth. She hesitated, then nodded. Her face was nearly white. Even her lips had paled. Her blond hair was tucked, for once, entirely beneath her bonnet.

"No, sir," Roger spoke up again. "Only I did. She scolded me after."

Elizabeth and Roger exchanged a quick look, too quick for Sarah to read either one of their faces. Had they planned this? She studied Elizabeth, staring at her dear, familiar face. No. Elizabeth was frightened, but there was also surprise in her eyes. She had not known that Roger was going to lie.

Sarah closed her eyes. The meetinghouse was cold, but she could feel a sheen of perspiration on the back of her neck.

"I admire truthfulness," Reverend Terrence was saying to Roger, "if that's what this is. But I condemn your acts." His face was hard, sharp. "Five stripes and five hours in the pillory."

Sarah gasped and she saw Elizabeth swaying on her feet. Five stripes? Men who stole or drank themselves stupid in public got whipped. She looked backward, trying to see her father's face, but he tightened his hand on her shoulder and held her still, facing Reverend Terrence.

"For Elizabeth," Reverend Terrence said, his voice heavy with finality, "a time equal to her brother's in the pillory. It will be done at ten o'clock this very morning," he added, his dark eyes fixed on Sarah's. "While the day is not so cold as to make them take ill."

Sarah saw Elizabeth's father fighting to stay calm. The punishments were too severe, Sarah thought frantically. Far too severe. She tried to speak, to master her aching throat and her fear, but her father was already turning her around, pushing her firmly from behind, guiding her toward the meetinghouse doors.

CHAPTER NINE

Outside the meetinghouse, Sarah stumbled along in front of her father. She wanted to scream the truth. She wanted to wrench from beneath her father's hands and turn back to shout into Reverend Terrence's face. She wanted to comfort Elizabeth and to thank Roger for his bravery. She wanted to run away forever, to find a place where people were not punished for laughter.

"John Hartford!"

Sarah felt her father's hands tighten and she stopped. The Watchman was leaning out of the meetinghouse doors. His dark clothing made him seem part of the doorway, as much a part of the meetinghouse as the snow-stained clapboards or the dark threshold stones. He cupped his hands around his mouth. "Bring your daughter back at ten o'clock. Reverend Terrence says she is to witness the punishments."

Sarah's father nodded, waving to show he understood. Then he started walking again, pushing her along, holding her steady when her balance faltered.

"We shall find Mistress Goddard," he said as they neared the road that ran along the edge of the commons. Sarah whirled around, startled out of her confusion. "I would . . . Father, please. I would rather . . ."

Her father nudged her back into walking. "You will do as I say." Sarah stumbled and he righted her. "Keep your feet, Sarah. Walk." His hands were firm on her shoulders, but she heard the sound of impatience he made deep in his throat. "Walk now, or I shall let you fall like a child."

He released her, and for a moment Sarah really thought she would fall. But then, somehow, her legs found their strength, and she made her way along the commons, following the road toward town. Once she was walking steadily, her father stepped around her to lead the way. Sarah breathed slowly, the cold air harsh in her lungs. Nothing seemed real. None of this should be happening.

"Mistress Goddard will talk to you about your friendship with Elizabeth," her father was saying. "As a mother would."

Sarah felt almost sick. Mistress Goddard was not her mother. Her mother had been gentle, with a soft voice and warm hands and a quiet, merry laugh.

"Sarah," her father said. He was pointing to the left. "You know the way."

Sarah led the way onto the familiar path that led into the clusters of houses beyond the commons, remembering herself at six years old, walking next to Elizabeth and Roger. They had walked this path every day they had gone to Mistress Goddard's dame school.

"Father . . ."

"I will hear no more foolishness," her father said flatly over his shoulder. "I have tried to do right by your soul and your character. But I have let you have too much your own way."

Sarah heard the sadness in his voice.

The snow was deeper here, sheltered from the wind by the hill behind the houses. Mistress Goddard's house was larger than those on either side. Her husband had been a joiner and a carpenter. Sarah paused, looking at the path leading to the door. It was narrow now, without the daily traipsing of children's feet to wear it wide and smooth. The snow had drifted across it in several places. Sarah hesitated. It had been three years since she had been inside this house. Her father nudged her again and she found herself walking toward the door.

"Mistress Goddard bore five children," her father said quietly.

Sarah, jolted out of her thoughts, looked back over her shoulder. "But she has none."

Her father nodded. "Pox. Fever. One daughter drowned at four."

Sarah faced the bleak wooden door. Little graves with tiny crosses were common. Her own mother had lost two babies before *she* had been born. It was a sorrow many women had to bear. She tried to feel sorry for Mistress Goddard, but she couldn't.

"We intend to marry," her father said, tapping at the door. Mistress Goddard opened it almost immediately, as though she had been standing near it, waiting. Sarah looked down at her shoes, absorbing what he had said. Marry. *They were going to marry.*

"Come in, John. Come in, Sarah."

The use of her father's given name, along with Mistress Goddard's soft tone of voice, startled Sarah into looking up. Mistress Goddard was smiling. Her face was transformed by the smile; she looked different, unfamiliar.

"I hoped," Sarah's father was saying, "that you would talk to Sarah about . . ." He made a vague gesture with his hands, then explained what had happened at the meetinghouse. Mistress Goddard listened attentively.

"Come in and sit," she said quietly when he had finished. Sarah followed her gesture. The students' benches had been taken out of the Goddard keeping room. Now it looked as most people's did. There was a long narrow table with backless benches on either side and another bench near the hearth. Ladles and spoons hung from a rack beneath a row of pewter porringers.

Mistress Goddard was still pointing to the bench nearest the hearth. Reluctantly, Sarah went to sit upon it, folding her hands in her lap to keep from wringing them over and over. She had meant to tell the truth. Now the lie was worse. Her father stood, talking in an urgent whisper at the door. As he spoke, Mistress Goddard nodded gravely, looking up once or twice at Sarah.

Sarah could not hear what her father was saying, but it was not hard to guess. He was convinced Elizabeth and her whole family were a terrible influence on her. She was his only daughter, his only child, and he wanted to make sure that she grew up to be a good Puritan and a good wife. And he wanted her to begin thinking of Mistress Goddard as her stepmother.

Sarah shifted on the bench and clenched her hands into fists. They were going to marry. And there was absolutely nothing she could do about it. Sarah felt sick. It was warm so close to the hearth. But she did not want to take her coat off, didn't want to look as though she wanted to stay in this house, even for a few minutes. She took off her gloves and laid them on the bench seat.

"I will return then, in a little while," Sarah heard her father saying. She looked up, automatically coming to her feet. But her father was motioning her to sit back down. Then he nodded briskly. "I will come back for you and we will attend the punishments, as Reverend Terrence bade us. In the meantime, you will stay here."

Sarah shook her head, but he silenced her with a sharp gesture and turned for the door. Once he was gone, she looked at Mistress

Goddard nervously. How could he do this? How could he leave her with the one person she least wanted to be with on this awful morning?

Mistress Goddard was smoothing her skirt and straightening her bonnet. "Sarah," she said, crossing the room. "Sarah." She sat down, just far enough away on the bench so they could face each other. "Your father is concerned."

Sarah didn't respond and Mistress Goddard didn't seem to care. She kept talking. "He has asked me to advise you. As a woman would. As a mother would."

Sarah fought to keep her face calm, to keep her feelings hidden. "It will be hard for you to watch Elizabeth punished," Mistress Goddard said evenly. Sarah did not even nod. She pressed her lips together.

"Elizabeth's family is under the eye of the ministers now. Did you know this?"

Mistress Goddard's words surprised her into reacting. Without meaning to, she answered. "The ministers?"

Mistress Goddard nodded knowingly. "Oh, yes. Her father and two of the sons have been fined for owning books no Puritan should read. And her mother often wears silk."

"But Elizabeth's father is wealthy," Sarah

objected. "His wife doesn't dress above her station."

Mistress Goddard smoothed her skirt again. "Perhaps not. But she is somewhat too concerned with worldly goods, you must agree. And so is her daughter."

Sarah shook her head. "Elizabeth prays everyday as she should. She . . ."

"Wears clothes that are much too fine. Her shoes . . ."

"What is so important about her shoes?" Sarah exploded. Immediately, she lowered her eyes, afraid of the flash of anger she had seen on Mistress Goddard's face, terrified of the anger she had felt in her own heart. She mumbled an apology, but the silence stretched out, filled only with the crackle of the fire on the hearth and the muffled sound of her pulse in her ears.

It was true that Elizabeth's parents were less strict than most. But even strict parents would have been able to find little fault with Elizabeth as far as chores, manners, and disposition were concerned. Elizabeth was going to make a wonderful wife and her husband would be envied.

"Sarah, look at me." Mistress Goddard's voice was terse, her face cold, familiar again. Sarah was sweating inside her coat now and her face felt flushed.

"Reverend Terrence gave the punishments he did because Elizabeth's whole family needs a lesson," Mistress Goddard said primly.

"It isn't fair," Sarah heard herself say. Then she pressed her hand against her lips. It would do no good to argue.

Mistress Goddard's face darkened with fury. "Do not speak against the ministers, Sarah. Your friend has dangerous ideas. Her whole family does. Roger discusses scripture with Reverend Terrence. He sometimes *disagrees*. And he has not yet even entered Cambridge College."

"But he will," Sarah said quietly. "And he is a good scholar."

Mistress Goddard shook her head. "He might never enter. People do not wish to pay their share to educate such minds." She stared into Sarah's face as though she was trying to find something hidden. "Nor will his father's money buy his way in if the ministers think him unfit."

Sarah sat very still, squeezing her hands into fists. Why couldn't Mistress Goddard just leave her alone? She needed to think, to sort out what to do next. More than anything, she wanted Mistress Goddard to stop talking. But the lecture wasn't over.

"Sarah, it is necessary for all of us to think

long and hard about those we call our friends."

Sarah turned aside to avoid the searching stare.

"Elizabeth and her brother have earned their punishment." Mistress Goddard insisted. "Roger must learn respect."

Sarah's heart was seething. Roger's only crime was kindness in lending her his coat.

"It is respectful to look at the one speaking to you," Mistress Goddard said. She reached out and took Sarah's chin in her hand and held her there, staring into her eyes. "Your father has told you that we are going to marry," Mistress Goddard said slowly. "I will expect you to behave as a proper young lady." Sarah swallowed, painfully. Mistress Goddard's hand was hard and tight on her chin.

"You will learn to obey," Mistress Goddard insisted. "No proper Puritan girl needs a friend who flirts with dangerous ideas. Such a friend is, in truth, an enemy of your soul."

Sarah tried to shake her head and Mistress Goddard tightened her fingers. "No. Do not disagree with me, Daughter."

Sarah wrenched herself sideways. Mistress Goddard leaned forward, grasping at her. Sarah broke free. She caught her skirt on the side of the bench and jerked it loose. She heard the cloth tear and Mistress Goddard's voice in the same instant.

"Sarah!"

Sarah shook her head, backing up. "Marry my father if you will," she heard herself say. "But I will never be your daughter." She wanted to say more. She wanted to tell Mistress Goddard Elizabeth was the best friend anyone could ever have, that Roger was kind and wonderful. But her throat had closed, painfully, tightly; her words were still trapped.

Mistress Goddard took a step toward her and Sarah whirled around and ran to the door. Hands shaking, she fumbled at the thumb latch and yanked the door open, running out into the glaring gray light of the cold morning.

CHAPTER TEN

Sarah ran up the path, nearly falling as she turned the corner, veering back along the edge of the commons pasture. She expected to hear shouting at any second, Mistress Goddard's voice shrill and angry, but she did not. There was only silence behind her as she ran, lifting her skirt to keep the heavy cloth from tangling around her legs. The only sounds were her muffled footfalls in the snow and her own heaving breath.

At first, Sarah ran to get away from Mistress Goddard, then she ran because she didn't know what else to do. She followed the path up the rise she and her father had come down, then on around the curve that brought it close to the forest's edge.

When she could run no farther, Sarah dropped back to a clumsy walk. Her breathing was harsh, the cold air thin and sharp in her lungs. She looked around wildly, then stopped, amazed at how far she had come. She was near the end of town, not far from the path that cut across the commons to the meetinghouse.

For a few seconds, Sarah stood still, staring across the uneven snow. There were a number of people walking toward the meetinghouse. The Tithingman had no doubt called upon nearby households to come witness the punishments. Sarah recognized the tanner and four or five of his older children. Perhaps his wife had been too busy to come. Or maybe she was ill? Goody Henshaw, who was probably the best dyer in the town, walked with her son's wife, their skirts an identical rich scarlet.

Her throat still aching, Sarah watched the people stream toward the meetinghouse. The whole town would not come, but many would. Some would be as angry as Reverend Terrence that the Sabbath had been broken. Others would be there only because it was an excuse to stop their work or because they disliked Elizabeth's family. A few, like old, fussy Goodwife Falset, loved to lecture wrongdoers.

Sarah blinked. Across the commons, she saw a little group of figures making their way to the meetinghouse. She recognized them instantly, even at this distance. They were alone, a wide space separating them from the others, a tall man leading a girl and boy who walked close together. The girl had on a yellow skirt and walked awkwardly, obviously wearing pattens. Sarah stood still, watching. Elizabeth and Roger were following their father back to the meetinghouse. Their mother had not come, nor any of their brothers. Sarah was glad. Elizabeth's mother would have been deeply upset if she had had to watch, or wait at home alone.

Sarah lifted her eyes to the trees, the dark edge of the forest. She could almost see the turnoff to the old Indian Road from where she stood. She forced herself to look back across the commons. Elizabeth was leaning on Roger, and he was bent close, talking to her. They did not see Sarah and her eyes stung with tears. She started toward them.

Sarah walked fast, refusing to let herself think about what she was doing. When she finally glanced up, she was more than half the way across the commons. All around her, the paths crisscrossed, widening where they joined, and people walked closer together. Sarah saw Roger, his face grave, staring at her across the dirty snow. He put his arm around Elizabeth's shoulders, guiding her along.

Sarah faltered, but she did not allow herself to stop walking or even to slow down. Her second-best skirt swung heavily around her ankles with every stride. In spite of the cold, she was sweating from her run. Her bonnet itched against her damp forehead and her stockings prickled. She kept walking, ignoring the people she passed and their questioning stares. Everyone knew how close she was to Elizabeth.

Roger supported his sister as they climbed the stone steps. Their father followed them, then ushered them through the wide doors. Elizabeth did not look up, did not see her. Roger did not look back at her as they went inside.

Sarah stopped and stood, shivering. There were people ahead of her, and their voices drifted back to her, vague and muted as they filed inside. Those behind her streamed past. She saw Priscilla's father, without his wife or family. Perhaps the Tithingman had found him in town and told him to come. Goody Falset was among the last, turning back twice to look at Sarah before she disappeared inside, closing the weathered gray doors behind her.

Then Sarah was alone. The wolf's head looked down at her from the log wall, proud even in death. The meetinghouse doors looked enormous. She squeezed her eyes shut, still breathing hard. Roger was willing to take the blame she deserved, but that did not make it right. It was her duty to tell the truth, to stand beside her best friend. It was her *right*.

"Sarah!"

Sarah spun around at her father's shout. He was standing a long way off, at the far edge of the commons. Mistress Goddard was beside him, a dark shape against the snow.

"Sarah!"

Her father was running toward her, his coat flying awkwardly from his sides. His eyes met hers across the trampled snow that lay between them. "Sarah!" His voice struck at her ears. In a few heartbeats he would be close, too close, and then she might never find the courage to speak.

Sarah turned and ran up the stone steps. She flung the doors open. As she burst into the dim interior of the meetinghouse, Reverend Terrence and the Tithingman looked up.

Roger was facing them, standing with his shoulders squared. Her head down, Elizabeth was at his side. Watchman Barton stood just behind her. The meetinghouse was full of people. They sat on the prayer benches or stood in small groups along the walls. They were talking in low voices that rose and fell like an uneasy sea.

Elizabeth saw Sarah and cried out. Roger turned quickly and took his sister's hand, talking urgently as he held her still. Their father was standing alone, off to one side. His face was full of pain.

"Sarah." Now her father's voice came from just behind her. Without looking back at him she gathered her skirts and made her way through the crowd.

"Reverend Terrence," she said in a near whisper as she got close. She cleared her throat. "Reverend Terrence."

"Yes?" He looked surprised at first, then annoyed when he realized who had spoken. "This is a serious matter, Sarah. Your father will tend to you."

"Reverend Terrence." Sarah raised her voice. This time he met her eyes for a moment before he turned to the Tithingman and spoke quickly in a low voice. Sarah watched, glancing back. Her father had not followed her. He had closed the doors and stood near them. Mistress Goddard, her face impassive, was on his left.

Elizabeth had begun crying quietly, her shoulders shaking. She pulled free of Roger and came toward Sarah, her face strained, blotched pink over her pallor. They hugged, swaying. Elizabeth leaned against her and whispered, "Oh, Sarah. Look what I have done to all of us."

"You are not to interfere," the Tithingman told Sarah, pulling them apart.

"But I did it. Not Roger," Sarah said, her voice rasping painfully as the words scraped past the lump in her throat. The murmur of voices, which had risen, kept her words from carrying far. But Reverend Terrence had heard her.

"What are you saying?" he demanded.

Sarah faced him, trembling. For a moment she could not speak, then she saw Roger, his face calm, almost proud. Of her? Sarah caught her breath, then let it out slowly. "Roger did not break the Sabbath. I did." Sarah said it loudly. She wanted Reverend Terrence to hear her—she wanted them all to hear her.

Reverend Terrence's eyes narrowed. Sarah glanced back toward the doors. Her father stood as though he had been stricken. Maybe he would never look at her again with pride. But she had to do this. She had to.

She lifted her chin, forcing herself to speak slowly and distinctly. "I was wearing Roger's coat. And so Mistress Goddard thought it was he."

In the sudden silence Sarah heard her father make a low, unhappy sound deep in his throat. When she glanced at him, he was looking back toward the doors, to where Mistress Goddard stood with her back to the wall, her hands smoothing her skirt over and over. The murmurs rose again as people close by began to understand what Sarah had said and repeated it to those who had not heard clearly.

Reverend Terrence raised his hands and called for quiet. Then he bent to look into Sarah's face. She swallowed. Her throat had closed again, swollen with fear. Reverend Terrence's face was set in righteous anger. He stared into her eyes. "Speak." It was a command.

In a painful whisper, Sarah told him what had happened and explained again why Mistress Goddard had confused her with Roger. She watched Reverend Terrence's face tense and darken. When he straightened, backing away from her, she was shivering, her knees unsteady.

It was over. Now she could only wait to see what he would do to her.

"We have," Reverend Terrence told the onlookers, "two Sabbath breakers, and a liar." He turned to Roger and shook his head. "What are you capable of? I should increase your stripes, but I will not." He glared at Elizabeth's father.

Sarah felt her heart racing as the two men looked at each other. Elizabeth's father refused to bow his head. Reverend Terrence finally snapped out a low order to the Tithingman. "We will need three pillories cleared of snow."

Sarah blinked back tears. Reverend Terrence was going to punish Roger anyway. How could he? Roger was going to be whipped. How would he be able to stand the hours in the pillory? How would Elizabeth? How would *she*? It was so very cold.

As the Tithingman left to obey Reverend Terrence, Elizabeth stepped toward Sarah and took her hand. They stood together, side by side, facing the people who lined the walls and filled the benches.

"Dear Sarah," Elizabeth whispered, "if you can be so brave, so can I."

CHAPTER ELEVEN

Once Reverend Terrence began the formal statement of their offenses, Sarah forced herself to look at her father. His mouth a thin narrow line, he was listening to Reverend Terrence.

"The Sabbath was broken in a willful and careless manner," Reverend Terrence said emphatically, using the pitch he used to carry his sermons to the back of the church. "There was play," he added after a tense silence. "Heedless laughter. Sliding in the snow." He paused again. "And this has been compounded by a lie." He gestured at Roger and explained how he had been willing to take a punishment meant for Sarah. The watchers exchanged looks and whispers.

"Or," Reverend Terrence said over the noise, "she is now lying for him." He gestured at Sarah and shook his head. "All three shall be punished."

Sarah clenched her hands, then wiped her suddenly sweaty palms against her skirt.

"All watching, learn from this example," Reverend Terrence instructed in a clear, clipped voice. "The girls, five hours in the pillory. For the boy, the same. And five stripes."

A murmur went through the watchers. Sarah glanced once more at her father and found him looking at her. For a few seconds, he only stared; then he turned and walked stiffly to the meeting-house doors. He paused long enough to say something to Mistress Goddard. Sarah could not tell if she answered him. Then he pushed open the heavy doors and went out. There was a flash of icy gray light; then the doors closed again.

Sarah blinked. Her eyes stung painfully. Elizabeth squeezed her hand. "Poor Roger," Sarah managed to say.

Elizabeth nodded miserably. "He wanted to spare you, and me, if he could."

Sarah fought the weakness in her legs. She looked past Elizabeth. Reverend Terrence was talking to Roger, whose face was resolute, composed.

Sarah watched Roger. His posture was rigid. His hands were stiff at his sides. There was a tiny muscle working in his jaw. Still, he kept his eyes on Reverend Terrence's face, apparently listening to every word the minister said. And when Reverend Terrence finished, Roger answered him.

Sarah could not hear Roger's words, but the effect on Reverend Terrence was immediate. He stepped back as though he had been struck. He looked over Roger's head for a long moment, then back down into his face. "We shall wait no longer," Reverend Terrence said to the people who lined the walls. He motioned to the Tithingman.

In a trembling daze, Sarah watched as the Tithingman and Watchman Barton took Roger's arms and walked forward, holding him between them. Roger kept his head high, but as he passed, Sarah could see a sheen of sweat on his face.

Elizabeth began to cry again. Sarah blinked, trying to hold back her own tears. There was nothing she or Elizabeth could do. She looked desperately for Elizabeth's father. Her hope died when she saw him, his face closed and remote, his hands thrust deep in his coat pockets. He wouldn't do anything. He *couldn't*. Reverend Terrence would never tolerate interference. There was nothing anyone could do.

"Outside now." Reverend Terrence was suddenly close, leaning to speak near her ear. Sarah flinched away from him. He frowned, regarding her. Then he raised his voice and repeated it to the watchers. "Outside."

Reverend Terrence put one hand on Sarah's shoulder and the other on Elizabeth's. Still holding hands, they walked unsteadily ahead of him, moving down the aisle behind Roger and the Tithingman. The people in the pews and along the walls, their familiar faces remote, expressionless, were staring at them. Goody Henshaw clicked her tongue and Sarah felt a rush of anger.

The Tithingman pushed open the doors and the glaring gray light leaped at them. Sarah shivered. Behind her, people began to move, pulling their coats higher around their necks, shifting their weight from foot to foot to warm up.

Elizabeth and Sarah followed the Tithingman as Roger was marched toward the whipping post. Reverend Terrence walked close behind them. All around them Sarah heard voices getting louder as people left the meetinghouse and came outside. Tears flooded her eyes and wet her cheeks, almost painfully cold in the winter air. Reverend Terrence guided them off to one side. "Stay here." It was another order.

Reverend Terrence gestured to the Tithingman, who turned and said something to Roger. Roger took off his coat and gloves, then untied his shirt and slid his arms out of his sleeves, baring his back. The Tithingman produced a leather thong.

Sarah felt faint. Elizabeth put an arm around her, but she, too, was shaking. The Tithingman bade Roger to the post and tied his hands above his head. Then he stood back and took a deep breath.

Without warning the Tithingman swept his arm up and lashed out with the thong. The sharp, cracking sound split the still air. Instantly, a long red weal rose across Roger's shoulders. The Tithingman raised his arm again and the thong cracked once more, raising another ugly red welt. The third stripe made Roger cry out, but the cry was muffled, bitten off. Sarah dug her fingernails into her palms. How could they do this?

The Tithingman stood straight for a few seconds, his face set, unhappy. Then he lashed out again. The fourth stripe brought a film of blood to the surface of Roger's skin. He made a small groaning sound, deep in his throat. Elizabeth echoed it, more softly, leaning on Sarah's arm. The fifth stripe, Roger bore in silence, but his body shuddered as the blood rose and beaded on the long welts. Her eyes tortured, Elizabeth took in a great, uneven breath.

Sarah forced herself to look away from Roger

and found herself looking at the crowd. No one was talking now. She spotted Elizabeth's father, off to one side, his arms crossed on his chest, his face invisible beneath his hat brim. She scanned the faces a second time. Her father was not there. Mistress Goddard, her face hard, almost smug, was.

The Watchman appeared at Roger's side and helped the Tithingman free his hands. They held him upright for a few seconds, but then Roger shrugged them off and stood on his own. After a moment the Tithingman helped him put his shirt back on, then his coat. Roger thanked him politely. The Tithingman nodded without expression and stepped back.

Elizabeth sagged against her and Sarah braced herself, trying to support her friend. "I am sorry," Elizabeth whispered, standing straight again after a moment. "I cannot . . . I am so . . ." Elizabeth stood still, looking at Sarah, tears running down her cheeks. "I am so . . . *angry.*" The last word was a bitter, hissing whisper and Sarah nodded. She was angry, too. She might never have admitted it, but she was. It was much easier to be scared. To be angry required courage.

Sarah held Elizabeth's hand tightly. She wanted to run, to pull Elizabeth with her, but running made no more sense now than it had at Mistress Goddard's. Sarah glanced at the little crowd again. Mistress Goddard was still standing, watching, well back in the crowd. When Sarah's eyes met hers, her expression did not change.

"Come." Startled, Sarah looked up. The Tithingman was beside them.

Elizabeth was trembling so violently that Sarah was afraid she might not be able to walk. How much of her friend's emotion was fear and how much anger, she could not guess. Elizabeth had paled until her skin looked like milk, but she walked steadily. Sarah looked past her friend to the pillories—and her stomach wrenched tighter.

The Watchman was positioning Roger's bare wrists in the rounded notches of the bottom pillory board. Roger bent forward quietly, unresisting. The Watchman lowered the top board, its notches matching the ones in the board below to entrap Roger's hands. Then he ran the lock rod through the bracket. Next he guided Roger's head down, so that his throat rested on the semicircle shape cut out of the head board. Roger's hair fell into his eyes and Sarah wished she could brush it back out of his face for him.

"Come," the Tithingman commanded. He led her to the center pillory, then positioned Elizabeth on the end. "You first," he said, facing Elizabeth. She looked up at him. "Your hands," he said, reaching out toward her. "Take off your gloves."

Shaking, Elizabeth obeyed and extended her hands. The Tithingman pulled her firmly forward, resting her wrists in the half-moon cutouts in the bottom board.

"Don't move them," he warned. A second later, he lowered the top board, clacking it into place, running the lock rod through. Sarah watched, trembling. Elizabeth was weeping again. Fear? Helpless anger? Hot, stinging tears welled up in her own eyes.

"They deserve it, they do."

It was a man's voice Sarah didn't recognize. Someone answered him, a woman. Mistress Goddard? Sarah tried to see, half turning, stopped by a sudden hand on her arm.

The Tithingman was beside her. She reluctantly raised her wrists. The wood was cold and rough against her skin. Someone in the crowd shouted something, but she couldn't understand the words. Then the Tithingman cupped the back of her head and was pushing her forward. Forward and down.

Sarah closed her eyes. The watchers' voices stopped, or, at least, she could no longer hear them. She could feel only her own pounding heart. The lock rod clattered into place. She was trapped. She could not move. And no one would dare help her.

CHAPTER TWELVE

Sarah could see people directly in front of the pillories only if she jutted her chin upward and tipped her head back, straining her neck. Most of the onlookers were leaving, walking in twos or threes.

Sarah turned a little to the side to look at Elizabeth. She had stopped crying. Beyond her, Roger was looking straight ahead, his face composed. Sarah closed her eyes. The darkness was comforting, like a calm touch.

"Sarah?"

Sarah twisted to look at Elizabeth. Her neck muscles strained to hold the awkward position.

Elizabeth's eyes were red from crying. "Forgive me."

Sarah wanted to shake her head, an impossibility in this position. "Do not blame yourself."

Elizabeth smiled faintly. "What a good friend you are."

They looked at each other for a long moment. Elizabeth's smile widened a little. "This is painful. I wish I had taken off these silly pattens."

Sarah tried to nod and banged her chin on the planks. It startled her and she gasped, wincing. Elizabeth winced with her. "Are you hurt?"

Sarah sighed. "No. Only foolish."

Elizabeth sighed. "They took our gloves."

Sarah realized that she had left her own at Mistress Goddard's. Sudden laughter made her raise her head. Almost everyone had gone. Only a few of the boys remained, poking each other and making jokes. And, of course, there was bitter-faced Goodwife Falset, ready to deliver her usual lecture. Sarah was grateful that it was too cold for casual watchers. In the summertime, there would have been many more to lecture them, to taunt them, and maybe even throw rotten food. Goody Falset cleared her throat and began to speak of the sin they had committed.

Sarah listened for a long time. Goody Falset

was right about many things. They had known what they were doing, and they had done it anyway. Sarah closed her eyes and prayed, asking for forgiveness. It was hard to concentrate with Goody Falset's high voice so close, so sharp.

Boys' laughter rang out from behind Sarah. So. The boys had not left. Maybe they'd lose interest before Goody Falset finished. Sarah turned her head to look sideways, past Elizabeth, at Roger. Was he listening to Goody Falset's voice, her shrill account of their wrongs? He had closed his eyes, his face still, peaceful. She wanted to thank him for trying to protect her. But she didn't want to say it in front of Goody Falset or any of the boys. Roger was so still. Was he praying?

"Ho!"

The voice was sudden and loud, followed by a volley of sharp laughter. A snowball exploded against Roger's cheek. He did not cry out, but his whole body jerked, his reaction restricted by the pillory, and he was startled into opening his eyes.

Taunts disrupted Goody Falset's recitation as two more snowballs flew past the head board. Neither hit Roger and he did not react. Sarah turned, trying to see who had done it. The first voice had sounded like one of the Callant brothers.

They all were rude; the eldest was a bully.

Ugly laughter from just beyond her vision made her twist again, and she felt a stinging pain where the rough board rubbed her cold skin. The boys were trying to stay just out of her vision, but she managed a glimpse. There. It *was* Harvest Callant and his brothers—perhaps a few others as well.

Goody Falset had paused. Now she started up again, but the boys' calls and shouts overshadowed her words as a snowball shattered against the side of Roger's pillory. Goody Falset began once more, but the rude laughter shoved her words aside. She glared, rubbing her gloved hands together for warmth.

There was a sudden whoop and five or six snowballs flew, all at once, most missing wildly. One hit Roger in the forehead. Sarah could see him blinking to clear his eyes.

Abruptly, Goody Falset turned to leave. Sarah watched her go, stumping toward the hemlocks and firs, following a path that went along this edge of the commons. Once she was gone, another volley of snowballs rained upon Roger. The taunts became louder now, more crude.

Sarah tilted her head back painfully. The boys were like dark crows circling carrion. Their shadows flickered across the uneven snow. They had spread out now, no longer cramped by Goody Falset's presence. Sarah saw a quick movement, an angular arm cocked, then released.

"Here's another, Roger!"

Elizabeth's whole body jerked at the sound of the voice. The snowball just missed, the spray of icy white streaking the board beside Roger's face. A second one shattered against the dark wood, hitting hard enough to crack like a musket. Sarah clenched her hands. They were putting rocks inside.

"Stop it!" Elizabeth shouted suddenly, her voice shaky and uneven. She struggled against the pillory for a few seconds, then slumped. There was more harsh, jagged laughter, then another snowball. This one hit Roger squarely in the face. He blinked to clear his eyes of snow. Sarah could see a little trickle of blood at the corner of his eye. She struggled against the pillories. This was wrong. She had seen people punished all of her life and had never thought about it very much. But it was wrong. These cruel boys had no right to hurt Roger. He was better in his heart and soul than any of them.

Sarah watched, helplessly, as the boys threw snowball after snowball at Roger. Most of them missed, but a few struck him full in the face. He lowered his head a little, but did nothing more. He would not answer their taunts. They circled, staggering with laughter at the misses, at Elizabeth's protest. Their taunts echoed in the woods.

After a time, with no reaction from Roger, the boys' sharp voices began to sound out of place among the silent trees. With fewer shouts and less force, the boys tried throwing at Elizabeth and Sarah. But when the first few snowballs missed, they began to drift farther away. One last snowball slammed into the pillory board near Sarah's face. She managed to turn her head a little, and she did not cry out when the ice peppered her stinging cheek. But she wanted to. These boys were the ones who should be punished. They took joy in another's pain.

Sarah could hear Elizabeth's harsh breathing and knew she was fighting to control her anger. Sarah had to dig her fingernails into her palms again to contain her own. What was wrong with these boys? What was wrong with the ministers?

At last the boys walked away, turning back a few times to shout insults, then just to look. Finally, they were gone.

"Harvest Callant," Roger said into the

silence after the boys were out of sight. "The future governor and his honorable friends. He is jealous of my Latin."

Elizabeth laughed a little, a cracked, limping sound. "You should never have won the last essay competition."

Roger did not answer her. Sarah wanted to say something, but nothing that came into her mind seemed worth speaking aloud. The silence around them deepened, pooling like deep water in the blue shadows of the trees. Looking at Elizabeth, Sarah kept her head turned for a long time. Finally, Elizabeth smiled apologetically and straightened, wincing as she moved.

Sarah looked forward again, too, flexing her cold feet by rising to her tiptoes, then letting herself sink down until she was flat-footed again. There seemed now to be no sound at all. The cottony silence settled heavily in Sarah's ears. They were alone.

It was so cold. Sarah blinked, squeezing her eyes shut as hard as she could, then opening them again. The whiteness of the snow was painful. She clenched her hands, wishing for gloves. Her hands were getting numb—and her feet would be eventually, too. Her back ached from the unnatural bent-over position. Her shoulders hurt and her neck was already bruised and raw from rubbing against the rough, freezing wood.

Sarah closed her eyes again and silently recited alphabet rhymes. She was on *T* for the third time when Elizabeth's voice broke into her thoughts.

"Sarah?"

"Yes?" Gritting her teeth against the sharp scrape on her neck, she twisted to look at Elizabeth. Elizabeth's bonnet was off-center, the ties dangling askew.

"Will your father punish you when you get home?"

"I think so. He was angry enough to leave."

Elizabeth sighed, but did not answer. Sarah closed her eyes again. She was so *cold*. For a while she hummed hymns, awkwardly moving her feet as though she were dancing in a tiny closet. She tried to recall every hymn she knew.

All at once Sarah realized she had stopped moving her feet, had stopped humming. How long had she been here? A strange sleepiness was tugging at her mind. She fought it, working her fingers into loose fists. She tried to rub her hands together, but only the fingertips could meet, her wrists held too tightly in the pillory.

It began to snow lightly, small perfect flakes drifting to the ground in swirls. Sarah tilted her head, trying to follow first one flake, then another. Where they passed in front of the dark firs, she could almost keep track, but when the air currents lined them up with the meadow or the horizon, she lost them against the grayness.

Sarah's heart beat endlessly. Twice she started to say something to Elizabeth, then stopped. Elizabeth finally looked peaceful, her eyes closed, her weeping stopped. Sarah tried to recite the alphabet backward. After trying for a long time, she managed it.

The gray had deepened, Sarah thought slowly, opening her eyes. It was snowing harder. She licked her lips, astonished at how cold they felt to her tongue. She turned her head to look at Elizabeth, who was slack against the pillory, her head fallen forward, her eyes closed. Sarah stared at her friend, scared and helpless.

"Elizabeth?" she whispered.

Elizabeth opened her eyes, then closed them again.

Sarah fought to keep from pulling at the pillories like a horse fighting a hated rope. It was useless. She would only hurt herself. There was nothing to do but wait.

CHAPTER THIRTEEN

Sarah struggled to stay alert, but two or three times she coughed, only then realizing that she had slumped forward, choking herself against the pillory boards. She closed her eyes, drifting in the darkness behind her eyelids, then opened them, trying to clear her blurry vision.

The trees seemed to sway, moving without wind. Their shadows were longer now, a deep, bruised gray on the snow. As Sarah watched, one of the shadows moved toward her, sliding apart from its tree. She stared at it, confused.

"Sarah?"

She blinked.

"Sarah?"

Her father stood for a moment in front of her; then he circled the pillory and fumbled with the lock rod. Sarah found her breath coming faster. She heard the clicking of the lock as it released. A moment later the pillory yoke lifted from her neck.

"Father . . . ," she managed to say as he freed her hands. Then she lost her balance, her numb feet betraying her. A sharp pain in the center of her back made her gasp. Her father caught her and held her up, his arm around her shoulders.

"I am sorry," he said softly.

Sarah looked up at him, not understanding.

He shook his head. "I have been more pious than good," he said quietly. "More careful than brave."

Sarah tried to stand, wincing as the pain in her back stabbed at her again, stopping her movement.

"I have told Mistress Goddard that we will not marry," her father said, leaning close to her ear. "She was relieved, I think, after all this." He gestured vaguely at the pillories and straightened up. "She will be even more relieved with the decision when she learns I've let you out early."

Sarah's heart leaped, but she said nothing.

Her father was looking intently into her face. After a moment he pulled her gloves from his coat pocket and worked them onto her hands. Then he spoke again. "Wives are hard to find." Sarah nodded slowly.

"But perhaps having no wife is better than having a cruel one."

Sarah smiled, her cold cheeks aching. Her father had never talked to her this way. He settled her against the pillory, hooking her elbows over the top plank so that she could stand without his help. "Stamp your feet. Bring them to life if you are able. We must walk. I didn't bring the sled. Too many would have noticed."

Sarah watched him move away. He went to Elizabeth, first saying her name, then gently freeing her. "Do you think you can walk?" Elizabeth answered, but Sarah could barely hear her voice. Her father pulled Elizabeth's coat higher on her shoulders and supported her until she had found a way to lean on the pillory. He bent to unbuckle her pattens and put them in his coat pocket.

He freed Roger, talking to him in a low voice, then turned back to Sarah. "Can you walk?" Sarah nodded, then almost fell as she tried to take a step away from the pillories. She leaned on the dark wood again.

"I can walk, Sir," Roger said. His voice sounded distant, as though he were shouting into wind. Sarah looked at him. He was marching slowly in place and rubbing his hands together. She copied him, afraid at first that she would fall, one arm still across the pillory bar.

Sarah's father bent to pick up Elizabeth. She relaxed in his arms like a rag dolly, her head lolling back. Sarah felt a clot of fear forming in her stomach. "Is Elizabeth . . . ?"

He smiled reassuringly, then looked past her at Roger. "Your father will meet us on the road on the other side of the commons. We thought it best not to give Reverend Terrence further reason to dislike him." He shrugged. "You have been here less than the five hours. But it is too cold. Your sin is hardly worth a young life."

Roger was taking a few steps now, backward, then forward, moving slowly, but keeping his balance. "I am ready, Sir."

Sarah was working her hands furiously as she stepped in place. The cold was receding a little. There were faint pinpricks in her fingers and feet.

"I will help Sarah," Roger said, and walked slowly toward her as her father swung around and led the way, Elizabeth's expensive shoes gently bumping his leg as he moved. Sarah took a halting step on her own, then another, with Roger walking close beside her, his hand on her arm.

"Lying is wrong," Sarah's father said over his shoulder. Then he turned back to face the path, his voice softer, but clear. "I would have done the same for Sarah's mother." Still he did not turn around. Roger did not answer, but Sarah saw him smile.

Sarah's father carefully carried her best friend across the trampled snow and Roger walked beside her. The gray evening was closing around them. She was cold and tired and every muscle in her body ached. And she felt like singing.

Father says there will be no fine or
punishment for his letting us out early.
Reverend Terrence says now that he was about
to do the same, since the day had turned so
cold. Perhaps it is true. Priscilla told me this
morning that many in town thought his
punishments too harsh, especially for Roger.

Elizabeth is abed, but will be fine soon.
Father says I may go every day to read to her
and keep her company. Constant Helms has a
litter of white kittens and Elizabeth's mother
says I may bring one as a surprise in a few
days. Roger says I have grown up. Perhaps he
is right. I am no longer afraid and I have made
a decision. I do not want to live here forever.
My children will grow up somewhere where
there are no ministers to punish them for
innocent play. Roger says there are many such
places. He says the world is enormous. All I
want is a tiny corner of it. It does not seem too
much to ask.